:3-

y,

g

5

VICTORIAN
MANSION
FLOWER SHOP
MYSTERIES

Bloomed
to Die

Johnnie Alexander

Annie's®

AnniesFiction.com

Library of Congress-in-Publication Data
Bloomed to Die / by Johnnie Alexander
p. cm.
I. Title
                    2017943279

AnniesFiction.com
(800) 282-6643
Victorian Mansion Flower Shop Mysteries™
Series Creators: Shari Lohner, Janice Tate
Series Editors: Janice Tate, Ken Tate
Cover Illustrator: Bill Bruning

10 11 12 13 14 I Printed in China I 9 8 7 6 5 4 3 2 1

1

The murmur of cheerful voices, interspersed with laughter, trailed behind Kaylee Bleu as she examined the new shrubbery encircling the Old Cape Lighthouse. The other Petal Pushers, who had welcomed Kaylee with open arms when she moved to Turtle Cove the previous spring, knelt along the path to the keeper's cottage as they placed antique ship lanterns among the freshly planted pink and white begonias.

She should be helping them instead of going off on her own. But she needed a few moments of solitude to soothe her nerves. This was the biggest, most important event she'd taken on since buying The Flower Patch from her grandmother. However, Bea Lyons was on a monthlong transatlantic cruise with her sister, so she wasn't available to help or offer advice. The shop's reputation now rested solely on Kaylee's inexperienced shoulders.

The vibrant beauty of the *Ribes sanguineum* shrubs brightened the lighthouse foundation, but they wouldn't have been her choice. True, the clusters of deep pink flowers looked lovely against the gleaming white of the freshly painted lighthouse. But flowering currants thrived near forests, not here along the coast. At least the groom had chosen a native plant, even if it was out of place in the sea air.

Kaylee groaned inwardly when she thought about what might happen to the poor plants after the wedding day. The groom's wish may be her command, but it had also required her to transplant the bushes in summer while they were in full bloom instead of during dormancy as was recommended. Hopefully they would survive beyond the nuptials.

Kaylee deadheaded a few brown flowers and placed them in a bag she had attached to her belt.

"No debris allowed," she said under her breath. Not that it mattered. Only Bear was close enough to hear her. "And no expense spared. Isn't that right?"

The six-year-old dachshund sat up on his hind legs and barked his agreement. Kaylee scratched the top of his head, and his cheery polka dot bow tie bobbed as he leaned into her fingers. She laughed as he lost his balance and toppled over. A second later he was on his feet again and bouncing around like a rubber ball.

"We think alike, you and me," Kaylee said. "What was already here only needed a little tender loving care and a bit of pruning."

After a typical frigid winter and rainy spring, the foundation shrubs had been bedraggled and weathered. Then someone— probably a well-meaning volunteer—got carried away with the pruning. Since then, Kaylee had crossed her fingers for the shrubs, but to no avail. Not wanting to see the destruction of healthy plants, even if they appeared sparse and untidy, she had avoided the lighthouse when the nursery workers replaced them with these new bushes.

"And time," she reluctantly admitted to Bear. "They needed more time to recover than we have, since the wedding is tomorrow."

Bear didn't seem to share her gloom. Instead he rolled on his back, scratching his long body against the manicured blades of grass and waving his legs in the air. Kaylee half-heartedly wished she could plop on the ground with the same joyous abandon. If only she were still six and could get away with it.

Bea had a photograph of Kaylee—she must have been about that age—showing her sprawled on the lighthouse lawn, arms and legs all akimbo. It was a happy picture, a reminder of her idyllic childhood.

Kaylee had found the photo in an album a few months ago. Her grandmother had left it behind, along with other albums and family memorabilia, when she sold her business and home to her granddaughter.

The Flower Patch, Wildflower Cottage, and the photographs now belonged to Kaylee. Before Bea moved to Arizona to live with her sister, she had handed Kaylee the keys and christened her the keeper of their family history.

Perhaps it was time to take that role seriously. She should sort through the photos, arrange them in albums, maybe even frame a few. She could create a family tree collage. Draw it on—

"Yoo-hoo! Kaylee!"

The cheerful call cut into Kaylee's thoughts. She turned toward the voice and smiled.

Brooke Edgars walked toward her, both hands clasped around her fiancé's arm. The young couple, in their mid- to upper twenties, could have stepped from a fashion magazine cover spread. The skirt of Brooke's floral sundress swirled around her bare legs. Golden sandals strapped across slender feet and revealed the bright pink of her toenail polish.

This was the new Brooke, who had money to spend on clothes and fancy shoes and pedicures, but still shopped sales. She embraced the perks of having Orcas Island's most eligible bachelor fall in love with her, but she refused to abandon her roots.

Her fiancé was James Stratford: millionaire, descendent of early settlers, and destroyer of healthy shrubs.

"I'm so glad to see you here, Kaylee," Brooke said. "Isn't this the most romantic place in the world to have a wedding?"

"I'm sure it must be." Kaylee looked around. "As you can see, we're getting it spruced up."

"About time too." James was more casually dressed than Brooke, wearing khaki shorts and boat shoes. He held a sleek silver travel mug in his free hand. "Since the rehearsal dinner is tonight."

"This is the first chance we've had to be out here," Kaylee said. "Thankfully, the sun decided to shine today."

"I ordered it to." James beamed at Brooke. "Everything needs to be perfect for our special day."

From the expression on James's face, he adored his bride. Apparently even a snobbish know-it-all could be smitten.

Feeling a little guilty about her earlier thoughts, Kaylee waved her hand in the direction of the new shrubs. "It was very generous of you to donate all this landscaping."

"I just can't tell you enough how much we appreciate you and the other Petal Pushers," Brooke said, barely taking a breath. "Getting your fingers dirty and putting in all this effort to make everything look beautiful. I know tomorrow is going to be the most perfect day."

"We're happy to help however we can," Kaylee said. "After all, you're an honorary Petal Pusher now."

A shadow seemed to cross James's face, but it quickly disappeared as he flipped open the lid and sipped from his cup.

Kaylee mentally rehashed what she had said, but couldn't imagine she'd inadvertently caused offense. Maybe she had only imagined his brief annoyance.

"I couldn't ask for better friends." Brooke released James's elbow long enough to squeeze Kaylee's arm. "When I moved back here, the Petal Pushers welcomed me with the warmest hospitality and friendship. It was almost like I'd never left. And I'm so glad my grandmother was one of the founding members so I can tag along with the rest of you once in a while."

Kaylee couldn't help a smile as she remembered her own warm welcome into the charming community. It hadn't been that long since she made her own move to this cheery little town.

At the time, losing her teaching position at Seattle's University of Washington had been devastating. But now she was thankful she got to spend her days designing floral arrangements instead of writing lesson plans, and pass her nights with a good book instead of grading a stack of papers.

Bea had been a Petal Pusher all of Kaylee's life. Now her grandmother's friends were her own.

"I know exactly how you feel," Kaylee said. She looked past Brooke's shoulder. "Speaking of the Petals, here comes Jess."

With her typical enthusiastic smile, Jessica Roberts approached them with a bounce in her step. She was about ten years older than Kaylee and owned the Death by Chocolate bakery next door to The Flower Patch. In the past few months, the two women had become especially close friends.

Jessica greeted everyone then turned to Brooke. "I finished the gourmet truffles for tonight's rehearsal dinner earlier this morning. How about a tasting?"

Brooke shrugged one dainty shoulder as she smiled at James. "What do you say, sweetheart? Would you like a taste of chocolate to go with that tea?"

James paused before answering, as if the question required his fullest concentration.

"I think the honey in this tea is enough sugar for me. Why don't you go along without me?" he suggested. "Since I'm already here, I want to go up to the widow's walk." He gestured toward the top of the lighthouse with the silver cup. "Look over my domain."

"Your domain?" Kaylee asked, unable to hide the "did I hear you right?" surprise in her voice.

"He's teasing," Brooke said with a girlish giggle. "Aren't you, sweetheart?"

"Sure I am." He chuckled, but the falsity of the sound grated against Kaylee's skin. She didn't know what it was about James, but she couldn't like the man. She'd tried, she really had. But then something always happened. He may not have meant it, but his attitude made her feel more like an indentured servant instead of a good friend who was arranging their wedding flowers.

Apparently Bear shared her feelings. When James first appeared, the dachshund had toddled behind Kaylee on his short legs and stayed there. His rounded body pressed against the back of her shoes.

"Run along now," James said, disengaging himself from Brooke's clasp and kissing her cheek. "I'll come by in—" he paused to make a show of gazing at his substantial gold wristwatch "—say, half an hour."

"See you then, sweetheart," Brooke said. "Kaylee, would you like to come with us? I'm sure the truffles are decadent."

"No thank you. I still have a few more bushes to clean up. But remember to bring your grandmother's lace handkerchief by The Flower Patch later so I can incorporate it into your bouquet."

"I won't forget. Everything about this wedding is going to be perfect."

Kaylee and Jessica managed to exchange an amused glance without Brooke or James seeing them. Though Kaylee wasn't fond of James, without a doubt he was a lucky man to have won the heart of a woman as genuine and kind as Brooke. She knew Jessica felt the same way about the bride-to-be.

Brooke tore her attention from her fiancé and looped her arm through Jessica's. "Shall we go? I'm dying to taste those chocolates."

James watched the two women walk away, took another sip from his cup, and faced Kaylee. "My bride doesn't realize how busy she'll be after our wedding. Between dinner parties and entertaining out-of-town guests, she's not going to have time for your little garden club. What's it called? Pedal Puzzlers?"

"Petal Pushers," Kaylee corrected.

"Ah well. To-may-to, to-mah-to."

"Not exactly." After all, no gardening club would go by the name of Pedal Puzzlers. That sounded more like a cycling group that solved brainteasers. She tried not to laugh at the mental image that thought conjured up. Good thing she'd found that spark of humor too, because James's superiority had once again needled.

Green eyes weren't the only thing Kaylee had inherited from her Irish mother. She also had an Irish temper, though she usually managed to keep it under control.

"Shouldn't Brooke be the one to make that decision?" she asked sweetly.

"It's not a question of decision, but of time." James stressed the last word as if he were explaining the concept to a class of kindergarteners. "As my wife, her schedule will be extremely crowded."

"I hope it's never too crowded for her friends." The cheer Kaylee forced into her voice barely lightened her tone. "Now, if you'll excuse me, I need to get back to work. We don't want any brown flowers to mar the wedding day."

"Nothing must spoil it."

Kaylee gave him a grim smile and walked away with Bear close on her heels. James didn't move.

"It *was* my domain once, you know," he called after her. Kaylee pivoted to face him, a quizzical look on her face.

"Excuse me?"

"That is, it belonged to my family. Practically everything the eye could see from the top of that lighthouse."

She shouldn't say it—she knew she shouldn't. But she couldn't resist.

"And yet," she said calmly, "my father's tribe, the Quinault, were here even before that."

She didn't wait for his response, but strode away with as much dignity as her pounding heart allowed. Later she'd come back to the section of shrubbery she'd been working on before James and Brooke had interrupted her. For now, she needed to channel the poised nobility of her father's ancient people and quell the fiery energy of her mother's.

Once she was out of James's sight, Kaylee plopped on the ground. Immediately Bear hopped into her lap. She gratefully endured his doggy kisses, then straightened his colorful bow tie.

"Can anyone join this party?"

Kaylee glanced up then shaded her eyes against the sun. "Sure. Have a seat."

DeeDee Wilcox, who lived and breathed whodunits as the owner of Between the Lines mystery bookstore, gracefully lowered herself to the ground. "What did the irrepressible Mr. Stratford do now?"

"How do you know he did anything?"

"Didn't you know? I'm an expert in body language cues."

"Must come from reading all those mysteries you sell."

"Guess so." DeeDee plucked a blade of grass and twiddled it between her fingers. "I didn't hear the conversation, but it obviously wasn't a pleasant one."

Kaylee settled Bear in her lap and recounted the exchange. As she talked, she slid her hand along Bear's back. The feel of his smooth coat and the warmth of his body quieted her jangled nerves.

"Then I told him my father's family was here first," Kaylee concluded.

"You didn't." DeeDee clapped a hand to her mouth, her eyes sparkling.

"Maybe not in those exact words."

"No wonder he didn't answer me when we passed each other."

"Where did he go?"

"Inside the lighthouse." DeeDee's musical laugh lingered

in the air. "I guess he meant it when he told you he was going to survey his domain from the widow's walk."

"He's probably going up there to spy on us while we finish the landscaping," Kaylee replied. "After all, everything has to be—"

"Perfect," they said together then laughed.

When the laughter faded, a pleasant silence surrounded them. As if by tacit agreement, they stood and gazed toward the shore. After several days of nonstop rain, it felt luxurious to relax in the sunshine.

DeeDee bent down and plucked another blade of grass. "Is something bothering you, Kaylee?"

Startled at the question, Kaylee automatically shook her head. "Why do you ask?"

"It's what you said to James." DeeDee gave a small laugh. "It was funny, and he definitely deserved the comeback. But you're not usually a comeback kind of gal. I mean that as a compliment."

Kaylee focused her gaze on the ocean waters of West Sound that separated the bulk of Orcas Island from its westernmost peninsula. On the horizon, the shoreline of Deer Harbor rose above the waves, the blues and greens of sea and the browns and greens of land shimmering in the afternoon sunlight.

DeeDee was right. Kaylee seldom thought of a good retort right away. Even when she did, she usually kept it to herself. Something was bothering Kaylee. She might not be the bride, but all the plans for Brooke's perfect nuptials had given her pre-wedding jitters. That, and the fear that she'd fail. She never wanted her grandmother to regret selling The Flower Patch to her.

Suddenly Bear jumped up and raced as fast as his short legs would carry him to a flower bed near the foundation shrubbery.

"What in the world?" Kaylee rose to her knees.

As Bear disappeared into the bushes, DeeDee said, "I'm glad we haven't planted new flowers in that one yet."

Bear reappeared and proudly trotted back to the women, something gold and shiny hanging from his mouth. As he drew nearer, Kaylee shifted her gaze from Bear to the widow's walk high above her, but she couldn't see much of anything from this angle.

"What does he have?" DeeDee asked.

Kaylee scooped up the dachshund and removed the golden object from his mouth. "It's James's watch."

2

Kaylee glanced from the watch back to the widow's walk. She almost expected to see James peering over the wooden railing.

"You'd think he'd take better care of his possessions," Kaylee said. She examined the watch. "The glass covering the face is cracked now."

"Any tooth marks from Bear?" DeeDee held out her hand. "Let me see it."

After Kaylee placed it in her palm, DeeDee looked it over. "Perhaps he has a wardrobe of watches. If he doesn't want this one anymore, I'll take it home to Andy."

"What about finders keepers?" Kaylee joked. "It'd make a fancy collar for this little guy." She scooped up Bear and scratched behind his ears. "You'd like a gold watch collar, wouldn't you, boy?"

DeeDee chuckled and held the watch up to Bear's neck. "You'll need to add a few links first. Or put Bear on a diet."

"He has gotten a little chubby, hasn't he?"

"Just a smidge. Probably from begging too many treats from the tourists."

"He is popular." Kaylee occasionally wondered if the island's visitors came into the shop only to get acquainted with Main Street's favorite dog. But since almost all of them left with a purchase, she wasn't about to complain.

"I think I've been eating too many treats too," Kaylee continued. "Sometimes I wish Jessica's bakery wasn't next door to my flower shop. At least you have to cross the street."

DeeDee gave a good-natured snort. "As if that makes any difference."

"Every little bit of walking makes a difference." Still holding Bear, Kaylee took a few steps away from the lighthouse to get a better view of the widow's walk. If she had dropped a fancy watch while up there, she'd be looking over the railing. But there was still no sign of James.

"Odd, don't you think?" Kaylee mused.

"What's that?" DeeDee asked.

Kaylee gestured upward. "That James hasn't shouted to us. Warned us not to run off with his watch."

"We still could." A good-natured glint appeared in DeeDee's grayish-blue eyes. "Shall we make a run for it?"

"You and I know we're both too sweet and innocent to get away with that. Besides, James is probably on his way down."

"Or maybe he didn't realize he dropped it." DeeDee held out the watch to Kaylee.

Kaylee took the watch and glanced at the face again. The fall had apparently stopped the hands at exactly 11:21. For a reason she couldn't explain, a shiver ran up her spine. She returned her gaze to the widow's walk. A cloud had slipped in front of the sun, and a gray shadow dimmed the lighthouse.

"I think I'll take it up to him. Want to come along?"

"No thanks." DeeDee drew back in exaggerated horror. "Too many stairs for me."

"Come on. I haven't been up there since I moved here. It'll be fun." Kaylee made her voice sound as enticing as possible. "We can look over the Stratford domain."

"You're on your own, girlfriend."

Kaylee rubbed her chin against Bear's head. "I guess it's just you and me, kiddo."

"You can leave him with me if you want. I'll keep an eye on him."

"Thanks, but I'll take him. It'll be an adventure. And he could use the exercise."

"I hope he thinks so." DeeDee chuckled, then tickled the underside of Bear's long snout. "Wave to me when you get there."

"Will do."

With Bear nestled in her arms, Kaylee entered the lighthouse through the rear door of the keeper's cottage and made her way to the front entryway. She gazed up the circular stairwell but didn't see any sign of James. Nor did she hear any footsteps.

"I guess we're going up," she said quietly to Bear. "I hope my legs get us there because I don't think yours will."

About halfway up, Kaylee leaned her back against the wall and sat on the broadest width of the step. Bear wriggled out of her arms and managed to climb three more stairs before turning and staring at her. He cocked his head to one side as if to say, "What are you waiting for? There are more steps to climb. Adventure awaits!"

"Give me a minute to catch my breath, Bear. I should have carried a bottle of water with me instead of you."

Bear barked, scrambled up two more steps, and barked again. A slight echo resounded in the stairwell.

"I'm coming." Kaylee took a deep breath, then followed Bear up the stairs. His plump rear end wiggled as his back legs scrambled to get up each step. Kaylee waited patiently, appreciating his slower speed. If they moved at a leisurely pace, she reasoned, perhaps James would tire of playing "lord of all I see." Then she could return the watch without climbing all the way to the top, thereby conserving energy she needed for her work.

"Though I guess we shouldn't give up now," she said to Bear. "After all, DeeDee is waiting for us to wave to her. Let's get a move on."

She scooped up the dachshund and quickened her pace. When she reached the top and stepped out on the widow's walk, a freshening breeze from the sea cooled her cheeks. She inhaled the familiar scent, drawing it deep into her lungs then smiled so widely her cheeks hurt. The walk encircled the lighthouse tower, and James was out of sight on one side or the other. He could wait a moment or two more for his watch. For now, Kaylee only wanted to take in the spectacular view.

The warmth of the sun's rays invigorated her tired muscles. The lovely blues and untamed whites of the sky and the sea spread before her in panoramic glory. Waves crashed upon the beach, reaching and receding, reaching and receding. The tidal pull seemed to tug at something deep inside Kaylee, an ancestral memory of her father's people in their canoes upon that sea, upon that beach.

She laughed at her fancifulness, amused by her own giddiness at being so high above the earth.

The view was worth every single step on every single stair.

A movement on the beach caught her attention. Someone was running across the sand. The runner veered inland, following a path among the wild grasses.

After she watched the figure disappear, Kaylee turned her face to the sky to soak up more warmth. Up here, so high above the ground, worries shrank against the vast expanse of sky and sea. As far as the eye could see, all seemed well with the world.

Perhaps that's how James felt too. Maybe it wasn't the island he was claiming for his own, but the experience of being a part of something grander than oneself.

Bear squirmed, pulling Kaylee from her thoughts. "Or maybe he's a greedy snob," she said, but with a lilt in her voice that softened the words. "Let's find him, shall we? Which way do you suppose he went?"

Bear pranced in a tight circle, let out a cheerful yip, and scurried on his short legs around the top of the lighthouse.

"Wait for me," Kaylee called as the tip of his tail disappeared from her view.

A short second later, Bear's anxious barking broke the morning tranquility.

Kaylee picked up her pace. She rounded the curve and gasped.

James was sprawled on the walk, one hand clutching his shirt. His other arm stretched outward, his fingers reaching for the silver travel mug he'd been carrying. It lay against the lighthouse wall, and dark liquid stained the planks. Bear carried the lid in his mouth as he paced between James's fingers and his head, leaving tracks where he'd walked through the spilled beverage.

Conflicting thoughts crashed in Kaylee's mind, rooting her feet to the boardwalk. Her forensic training shuddered at Bear's movements—he was disturbing the scene—but another part of her brain refused to believe what she was seeing. Any second now, James would sit up. Or groan. He'd do something.

But he didn't.

Reconnecting with reality, Kaylee didn't have to get any closer to know for sure: The groom was dead.

Bear dropped the lid. He barked softly, then poked at James's ear with his nose.

"No, Bear," Kaylee said quietly. "Leave him alone."

Bear whimpered then lay down, resting his long nose on his front legs. He whimpered again.

Kaylee approached James and knelt next to his body. She placed a comforting hand on Bear's back then turned her attention to James. His face appeared contorted as if in pain, and his eyes stared at the sky.

"James," Kaylee whispered, even though she knew he couldn't hear her. She needed to call 911. To get paramedics here.

Brooke.

Someone had to tell Brooke.

Rapid-fire thoughts pounded against Kaylee's brain. She pulled her phone from her pocket, trying not to stare at James.

Even as she dialed, she knew the paramedics could do nothing for him now. But she could.

She leaned forward and gently closed his eyes, then sat back on her heels and prayed while she waited for someone to answer her call.

Kaylee and DeeDee waited for help near the doorway to the widow's walk, their backs against the lighthouse wall. Bear rested in Kaylee's lap.

After calling 911, Kaylee had phoned DeeDee, telling her about James and asking her not to say anything to anyone else. Not yet. The news would spread quickly enough—that's the way it was in a small town—but hopefully not until someone had a chance to talk to Brooke.

"I still can't believe it," DeeDee said. "James Stratford is dead. How is that possible?"

DeeDee had asked the same question, in different words, more than once since appearing on the widow's walk out of breath. But Kaylee didn't have an answer.

"I guess you never know," DeeDee continued. "He was young and healthy and still . . ." She shook her head. "Poor Brooke."

Kaylee started to answer, then tucked Bear beneath her arm. "I hear sirens. They're coming."

Both women stood and looked over the railing. From their vantage point, they could see the road leading into the parking lot. The emergency vehicles came into view.

Kaylee looked down. Only a little while ago, she'd been

tending the new shrubbery and talking to James and Brooke, the happily-in-love couple who expected to spend the rest of their lives together.

Now their perfect wedding would never happen.

"Here they are," DeeDee said, pointing toward the lot.

Sheriff Eddie Maddox, tall and physically fit despite nearing sixty, strode toward the keeper's cottage. Deputy Nick Durham, about fifteen years younger than the sheriff, followed close behind. Two EMTs, carrying a stretcher and medical bags, brought up the rear.

Kaylee and DeeDee returned to the body, and it wasn't long before the officers and the EMTs joined them. Everyone murmured greetings, and then the older EMT knelt beside James and checked for a pulse. He gazed at the sheriff and shook his head.

"What happened here?" Sheriff Maddox asked.

"We don't know." Kaylee hugged Bear a little tighter and he whimpered. "James told me he was coming up here to—" She stopped and shot a glance at DeeDee. The exact words didn't matter, nor did James's arrogance. Not anymore.

"He said he wanted to look around," Kaylee continued. "DeeDee and I were chatting, and then Bear shows up with James's watch. I guess it fell. I mean, it must have. He'd been wearing it."

Aware that shock was making her babble, she pulled the watch from her pocket and handed it to the sheriff. After examining the watch, he dropped it into the evidence bag Nick held open for him.

"You're sure Stratford was wearing it?"

"He checked the time when we were talking. I saw it."

"Then what happened?"

"He didn't come down, so eventually I came up." Kaylee closed her eyes to block out the horrific memory of that first glimpse of his body. "He was like this when I came up here."

"Did you touch him?"

"I closed his eyes."

"Anything else?"

"Bear had the lid to the cup in his mouth, but I didn't touch it. Eventually he put it down by himself." She fiddled with Bear's bow tie and realized the fabric was wet. Probably from James's tea. She wiped her damp fingers on her shorts. "All I did was call 911. And then DeeDee."

"Call anyone else?"

"No one." She met his gaze. "He's engaged, you know. He was supposed to get married tomorrow."

"I'd heard that."

Of course he had. Everyone on Orcas Island knew their millionaire bachelor had finally been caught in a nuptial net.

"Someone needs to tell Brooke."

"Someone will."

The sheriff glanced at the body then sighed heavily. "Any idea about cause of death?" he asked the older EMT.

"Can't say without an autopsy."

Sheriff Maddox exchanged a meaningful glance with his deputy, who nodded and stepped away to make a phone call.

"Ladies, we need to treat this as a crime scene." Before either of the women could respond, he held up both hands, palms facing them. "No doubt, Mr. Stratford died of natural causes, but we still have procedures to follow. If the autopsy reveals that it was murder, we will need as much information from the scene as we can get."

Bear's sausage-like body tensed in Kaylee's arms then seized. The convulsions surprised her so much she almost dropped him. She cradled him closer, her heart racing and her thoughts in a panic. The younger EMT was suddenly beside her. He took Bear from her shaking arms.

"Has he ever done this before, ma'am?"

Kaylee tried to speak but no words came out. She numbly shook her head.

The EMT pressed his fingers gently against Bear's chest. "He needs a vet. Now."

"What's wrong with him?"

"Can't say for sure." The EMT gazed into Kaylee's eyes. "But I think he's been poisoned."

3

Kaylee wrapped her arms around her tense body and stared at the giant poster of dog breeds hanging on the exam room wall. Each breed was listed under its native country or region. She and Bear had made it to the veterinarian's office in record time thanks to Sheriff Maddox, who had immediately instructed his deputy, Nick, to give Kaylee and Bear a ride in the squad car.

It had taken way too long to get down the lighthouse stairs and sprint across the grounds to the parking lot for Kaylee's comfort. But Deputy Durham made up for it. With siren blaring and lights flashing, they soon pulled up to the office door. He hadn't even shifted into park before Kaylee had jumped out, Bear's unconscious body in her arms.

Now the little dog was with his doctor, somewhere beyond this examination room, and all Kaylee could do was wait.

"Are you sure I can't get you anything?" DeeDee asked, putting a hand on Kaylee's arm. She'd driven her own car, and it had taken her at least ten more minutes to make the trip.

Ten minutes that might make a difference for Bear. Kaylee needed to thank the sheriff and Nick for helping her out. The sheriff would be easy. But with Nick, she'd have to be careful how she worded her appreciation. Otherwise he'd rope her into a date with him, something she'd carefully avoided until now. The man was an incurable flirt who never accepted defeat. "I'll wait," he was known to say when a woman refused to go out with him. Normally Kaylee didn't mind, but she wasn't in the mood when Bear was sick, possibly—no, she couldn't even think the word.

"Kaylee," DeeDee said softly.

With a quick shake of her head, Kaylee faced her friend and gave a grim smile. "Sorry. Guess I was lost in thought."

"Why don't you sit down?"

"I can't." She hugged her body and rubbed her arms. "When Grandpa's murderer tried to poison Bear, I stopped him. But not this time." Her eyes burned as that appalling moment replayed itself in her mind. The murderer pouring poisoned liquid onto the ground. Kaylee's quick command to Bear to leave it alone. She'd saved her sweet little dog then. She should have done the same for him now.

"You couldn't have known James's mug had poison in it," DeeDee said. "This isn't your fault."

Kaylee knew DeeDee was right, but she still felt responsible. Ever since she first saw Bear at the shelter, she'd promised to always look out for him. But she had failed. To distract her guilt-ridden thoughts, she searched the poster for Germany, and then she pointed to the side-view image of a long-bodied, stubby-legged, russet-brown dachshund.

"This one looks just like Bear."

"He's going to be fine." DeeDee stood beside Kaylee and rubbed her back. "Dr. Melody is a fine vet. She'll do everything she can for him."

"I know. I just wish I could be back there with him."

There was a knock on the door and Sheriff Maddox entered, followed by a veterinary assistant. The sheriff carried an evidence bag with James's silver travel mug inside.

"Where's Nick?" Kaylee asked.

"He went back to the lighthouse." The sheriff held up the evidence bag. "I know this is unorthodox, but the good doctor said we could use her equipment to test what's left in this mug. I'll still need to send it to the crime lab in Seattle, but it'll give us a head start. Maybe it'll help Bear. And my investigation."

Kaylee nodded in understanding. If the poison was plant-based, she should be able to identify it. "I can do the test?"

"As Turtle Cove's resident forensic botanist consultant, you may."

Kaylee slightly smiled at his attempt to lift her spirits. With a PhD in plant taxonomy, she'd helped the Seattle police on several cases in that capacity. She and the sheriff had a running joke about her fancy title. Though he'd been interested in talking about the cases she'd worked on, she knew he never expected to need her expertise here in quiet, laid-back, small-town Turtle Cove.

Not until now.

"If you'll both come with me." The assistant led them to a small corner room. The walls were lined with stainless steel countertops and cupboards. One section held lab equipment, including two microscopes.

DeeDee followed them, then stopped near the door. "I'll wait for you in the exam room, Kaylee. Otherwise I'll be in the way."

The assistant provided Kaylee with gloves, then gathered the needed supplies.

"Any news on Bear?" Kaylee asked, her voice hesitant.

"We pumped his stomach," the assistant said, "and we're giving him oxygen."

"That's good. Isn't it?"

"Dr. Melody will join us in a few minutes." He gave an encouraging smile. "She'll give you an update."

Kaylee nodded her thanks and busied herself preparing a slide. Sheriff Maddox removed the mug from the evidence bag and set it on the counter beside the microscope. Kaylee dipped a long swab into the dregs at the bottom of the mug, then transferred the brown liquid onto the slide.

If the drink was poisoned . . . Myriad possibilities flitted through her mind. It could be a chemical, but that trick required disguising the taste so the victim didn't notice that anything was wrong. Arsenic was a popular choice. But so were several toxic plants.

She took a deep breath, placed the slide on the tray, and peered into the scope. By adjusting the lens, she sharpened the image and identified the minute specks in an instant.

"*Nerium oleander*," she said. "The mug contains oleander."

"You're sure?" Sheriff Maddox asked.

"Positive. When I was teaching, I did a practicum on poisonous plants. I showed slides to my students that are identical to what's under this lens." She decided not to mention the case she'd been on. The father of a not-so-promising quarterback had spiked a rival's sports drink with crushed oleander leaves. Fortunately, that kid had survived.

Hopefully Bear would too. But it was too late for James.

"I'll tell Dr. Melody," the assistant said.

"Wait a sec." The sheriff's authoritative voice stopped the assistant from leaving. "This is now a homicide investigation, and this is a detail I want to keep private. Tell the doc so she'll know how to treat Bear, but no one else. Do you understand?"

The assistant nodded, his eyes wide.

"Go ahead then."

The assistant hurried out of the door as Sheriff Maddox bagged the mug. "Oleander," he muttered.

"Let me show you." Kaylee did a search on her phone and handed it to him. "Here are the images. It's an evergreen in the *Apocynaceae* family. They can get quite tall, as much as fifteen to twenty feet, and as you can see the flowers grow in clusters."

"Which part is poisonous?"

"There's no part of it that isn't poisonous."

Sheriff Maddox gave a low whistle. "So someone ground up pieces of an oleander plant—leaves, stems, whatever—and poisoned Stratford?"

"Looks that way. It couldn't have been the bees."

"The bees?"

Kaylee faced the sheriff. "I once read a report of bees making honey from the nectar of poisonous plants. I think in that case it was a rhododendron. The honey was tainted, and several people got sick and even died from eating it. They called it 'mad honey,' because people hallucinated when they ingested it."

Sheriff Maddox scratched his chin. "How do you know there is honey in that tea?"

"James mentioned it to Brooke when she asked if he wanted some of Jessica's chocolate truffles. He said the honey in the tea was enough sweetness."

"So how can you be sure this honey wasn't tainted by the bees who made it? Maybe the honey was made from oleander."

"The mug contained actual specks of an oleander plant. It wouldn't have done that if the poison was in the honey. And honey can't be made from oleander anyway, because it doesn't produce nectar."

"I thought honey was made from pollen."

"Nope," Kaylee said. "Bees do consume pollen and move it from plant to plant, but the only way it gets in honey is by accident."

"So oleander produces pollen, but not nectar. What if a bee accidentally transferred oleander pollen to the honey?"

"That's possible, but I saw actual bits of oleander plant, and too much for it to have been an accident.

"So in your expert opinion, the only way poison got in that honey was if a person put it there? We can't hold any bees responsible?"

Kaylee gave him an apologetic look. "It had to be deliberate."

"I don't suppose you have any ideas who did it?"

Kaylee couldn't begin to imagine. She supposed James had enemies, or at least there were people, including her, who didn't particularly like him. But who hated him enough to kill him?

She sighed heavily and met the sheriff's gaze. "I'll process this slide for you," she offered.

"Thanks." He handed her an extra evidence bag. As soon as she sealed it, they both signed and dated the exterior. "I take it you aren't going anywhere."

"Not until I know Bear's okay."

"What I said to that assistant goes for you too. The oleander remains our secret."

"I understand."

"Good." Sheriff Maddox straightened and adjusted his gun belt. "I'm going to step out and call the coroner. I want to talk to him before he starts the autopsy."

"What about Brooke?" Kaylee asked. "Has anyone talked to her?"

"She was the nearest thing to next-of-kin James Stratford had. Deputy Garcia found her at the bakery. Last I heard they'd gone to Brooke's home. Jessica Roberts is with them too."

"That's good." Kaylee didn't know Robyn Garcia very well. Only that she was a talented quilter who had once ordered several centerpieces for a quilting club luncheon.

"I'll be heading over there soon," Sheriff Maddox said. "I'd like you to come too."

"Me? Why?"

He hesitated, his dark brown eyes somber. "Well, she knows you, and you have experience with my side of law enforcement. I know you probably didn't do many interrogations when you helped the Seattle police, but I think Brooke would be more willing to talk with a familiar face in the room."

"Why do you want to question her anyway? Isn't she having a hard enough time?"

"You have to know the statistics. It's usually the spouse. And the wedding was only a day away."

"You suspect Brooke?"

"Not because I want to."

"I can't believe she'd do anything like that. What would be her motive?"

"Stratford was a wealthy man."

"But not until they were married"—Kaylee hesitated to gather her thoughts—"I mean, as his wife, she'd have more legal standing. As his fiancée? It doesn't make sense."

"We'll know more after we talk to her. Will you come with me when I go to question her?"

Kaylee's shoulders sagged as her thoughts whirled. Brooke couldn't possibly have poisoned James. If the sheriff had seen them together this morning at the lighthouse, he would know it just wasn't possible. Someone else had to be responsible.

But if not Brooke, then who?

For Brooke, this day had started out perfect. She was set to marry the perfect man, having planned the perfect wedding. Now all her dreams had been shattered by the tragic, unexpected death of the man she loved.

Her heart must be breaking, and to top it all off, now she was going to be questioned as if she were a common criminal instead of a blushing bride.

"Do you have to do this?" Kaylee asked quietly. "She was ready to promise him the rest of her life."

"It's my job. Like it or not, right now she's the first and only person on my list of suspects."

"I need to talk to Dr. Melody first."

"That's fine. I'll wait for you outside." Sheriff Maddox gathered the evidence bags, headed for the door, then paused and turned back. "Thank you, Kaylee. I know this is hard on you, and I'm sorry about Bear. But I appreciate your help."

Kaylee merely nodded. As soon as he left, the tears she'd been holding back streamed quietly down her cheeks. What would she do if Bear didn't survive? He'd been her companion since she first took him home. There had been several dogs at the shelter to choose from, but the instant she saw the little dachshund with the big heart, she knew they were meant to be together. And she'd been right.

He had to be okay. He just had to be.

As Kaylee tried to compose herself, Dr. Melody entered the lab.

"Is he . . ." Kaylee managed to get out before a knot clogged her throat.

"He will be just fine." Dr. Melody rummaged through a cupboard for a box of tissues and handed it to Kaylee. "Would you like to see him?"

"Please."

As they walked toward the recovery area, Dr. Melody gave Kaylee her prognosis. "He's a tough little guy with a strong constitution. But I'd like to keep him overnight, just as a precaution."

"That would be fine," Kaylee said as she spied Bear tucked into a bed that reminded her of a newborn's hospital bassinet. She gently ran her fingers along his back, careful to avoid touching the IV stuck into his leg. He whimpered quietly, and she scratched his head. For the first time since Bear had convulsed in her arms, her spirits felt lighter.

Bear was going to live.

Kaylee and Jessica sat on the couch, one on each side of Brooke, while the sheriff scribbled notes in a pocket-sized, spiral-bound notebook. Deputy Robyn Garcia, her light brown hair pulled back into a ponytail and the heel of her hand resting nonchalantly on her holster's safety strap, stood near the front window.

The news of James Stratford's death had swept through the close-knit community, and a couple of reporters leaned against their cars on the quiet residential street. They'd tried to get a statement from Sheriff Maddox and Kaylee when they arrived, but the sheriff had politely declined.

Kaylee hoped that with all the havoc going on in the world, the Seattle television stations wouldn't find a small-town murder newsworthy enough to send a crew. The last thing Brooke needed was TV vans parked outside her home.

Between bouts of tears, Brooke answered the sheriff's questions with a jagged voice. She and James had stopped in at the Pacific Street Diner to meet their wedding planner then had driven to the lighthouse.

"Just before we left the diner," Brooke said, "James poured my iced tea in the travel mug to keep it cold. Everyone knows my love for honeyed tea."

"For what?" Sheriff Maddox asked.

Brooke bit at her lower lip and choked back a sob. "I guess not everyone," she said in a low voice. "I put honey in my tea. Or as James would say, I add tea to my honey."

Jessica squeezed Brooke's arm then gave the sheriff a smile. "She adds honey to her tea, practically by the cup. Whenever she was over for a playdate with Mila, I always made sure I had honey on hand." Jessica gazed toward the window. "I'd say, 'Brooke, you're sweet enough without that honey.'" Jessica brushed away a tear, and her lips curled upward in a tender smile. "We even referred to the jar as Brooke's honey. We still do."

The sheriff waited a moment for Jessica and Brooke to compose themselves, then cleared his throat. "Who put the honey in the tea?"

"I did. I carry honey with me for that very reason." Through her tears, Brooke attempted a weak smile.

Sheriff Maddox stared at her until she dropped her gaze. "If the tea was for you, why did James have it?"

Brooke's eyes darted from her lap to the sheriff to the opposite wall. "He was carrying it for me. He was always a gentleman like that. Opening doors, pulling out chairs . . . he called it 'taking care of me.'" She took a deep breath, and when she spoke her voice was hesitant, unsure of itself. "I was so excited about going with Jess to try out the chocolates I forgot to take it with me. Besides, I think he started liking it almost as much as I do."

Kaylee tensed, her nerves suddenly on high alert. She caught Jessica's gaze and realized they were thinking the same thing. Had the murderer intended to poison Brooke instead of James?

"Do you still have this honey you always carry with you?" Sheriff Maddox asked.

"It's in my bag. Right over there." Brooke pointed to a nearby table.

"I'll get it," Deputy Garcia said. "If you don't have any objection, Ms. Edgars."

Brooke shook her head, and the deputy snapped on a pair of gloves. She opened the bag and pulled out a small glass jar about three-quarters full of amber honey. Holding it gingerly by the lid between two fingers, she offered it to the sheriff. He reached into his pocket and drew out an evidence bag.

"I don't think I've used as many of these things in the last year as I've used today," he said. Once he opened the bag, Deputy Garcia slid the honey jar inside.

"What are you going to do with it?" Brooke asked.

"Test it for any foreign substances," Sheriff Maddox said.

Brooke's face paled. "What kind of foreign substances?"

"The kind that kills people."

4

Kaylee sharpened the microscope's focus on the honey-laden slide and felt her stomach drop. They had returned to the veterinarian's crowded lab room to test the contents of the honey jar from Brooke's bag.

"Well?" Sheriff Maddox asked.

She caught his gaze and said softly. "There's oleander in the honey."

"You're positive?"

"I wish I wasn't." Kaylee rubbed her eyes with both hands as if to erase the memory of what she'd seen on the slide.

The sheriff tapped his hat against his leg and exhaled a long breath. "Never expected to see a day like this one."

"What happens now?"

"I'll take the morning ferry to Seattle. Stratford's travel mug and Brooke's honey jar need to be examined by the crime lab. No offense."

"None taken," Kaylee said. "Though I can't imagine anyone wanting to kill Brooke."

"Brooke?" The sheriff's eyes narrowed. "So you think she's the intended victim instead of my primary suspect?"

"Don't you?"

"I admit it crossed my mind. Just kind of hoped it hadn't crossed anyone else's."

"Sorry," Kaylee said sheepishly.

Sheriff Maddox waved away her apology. "Tell me why you think Brooke isn't guilty of killing her fiancé."

"If she killed James, why would she admit to having the honey jar? Or keep it at all? And again, why wouldn't she wait until she was his wife and would benefit financially from his death?"

"Misdirection. Or maybe she slipped up. Criminals are never as smart as they think they are."

Kaylee studied a framed poster of the anatomy of a cat while she considered the sheriff's suspicions. "I guess it's possible," she finally admitted.

"Your theory is possible too." Sheriff Maddox let out a frustrated sigh. "In fact, I hope you're right. Not because I want Brooke to have been the victim—I didn't mean that. But there's something especially diabolical about killing someone you're supposed to be in love with. On the other hand, if she had been the victim, I would have had to suspect James."

"She seemed so happy this morning," Kaylee said. "Not at all like someone planning a murder."

"She wouldn't be the first woman to fool her friends with an innocent act."

"I guess not." Kaylee turned away from the sheriff and removed the slide from the tray. What he said was true. Her colleagues on the Seattle homicide squad had told her a couple of stories of infamous "black widows." But Brooke and James hadn't even been married yet. What possible motive could she have for killing him?

"It's not always about the money," Sheriff Maddox said as if he'd read her mind.

"Jealousy, revenge, pride." Kaylee ticked off a few other popular motives as she placed the slide in an enclosed container. "Greed, needing to keep a secret, hatred."

Sheriff Maddox settled his hat on his head then took the slide. "Most days I love my job," he said. "I love keeping the public safe and upholding the law. But situations like this make me think about retiring. People can be so despicable."

"Are you going to arrest Brooke?"

"Right now, she's a person of interest. I'm going to take her in for more questioning." He paused at the door and glanced back at Kaylee. "Thanks for your help today. It's nice having a forensics expert around when you need one."

"I'm glad I could help." *I think.* In this case, she hoped that her involvement didn't lead to the arrest of a friend.

"No sleuthing on your own, though. We don't want a repeat of what happened the last time you got too nosy, do we?"

"Absolutely not." She gave him a grim smile at the unpleasant memory. He tipped the brim of his hat and left.

It wasn't like she wanted to be involved in this case. If Bear hadn't ingested the poison, Kaylee might not have been drawn into this investigation. She would have been back at The Flower Patch by now, literally minding her own business while Bear played or napped nearby. Thankfully Mary Bishop, the shop's part-time designer, was available to help any customers who might have stopped by.

Granted, Kaylee imagined the town's hot spot right now was either the Pacific Street Diner, where James and Brooke had met their wedding planner earlier in the day, or Jessica's Death by Chocolate bakery and coffee shop. Gossip would be the dish du jour at both spots.

If Kaylee went back to The Flower Patch, curious townsfolk would find an excuse to drop in to hear her account of what had happened. It might be prudent to ask Mary to close up so Kaylee could go straight home.

But first she needed to see Bear again. She'd stay with him as long as Dr. Melody allowed.

The next morning Kaylee stopped in to check on Bear and made arrangements to pick him up later in the day. She then joined the other Petal Pushers and several other local women at the lighthouse keeper's cottage to tackle the task of removing evidence of the never-to-be nuptials, including sending back gifts.

As Kaylee stepped into the cottage, she waved at Jessica across the room and then surveyed the scene before her. Fine china, crystal vases, and other luxury goods were piled on white-clothed tables throughout the living and dining areas. James had insisted on displaying his and Brooke's wedding gifts as they received them, showcasing the packages along with the greeting cards that had accompanied them. Kaylee and the others had rolled their eyes at his ostentatious request, but Brooke had found it endearing. She had shared her perspective with Kaylee when they last discussed the wedding flowers.

"I know it's a little much," Brooke had confided, her cheeks blushing with either embarrassment or pride—Kaylee wasn't sure which, though maybe it had been a little of both. "He wants everyone to know how happy we are, and I don't think he knows the best way to do that. He's always gotten everything he wanted, you know. He doesn't understand that some people find him arrogant."

Kaylee couldn't relate to a life of buying whatever she wanted without considering the cost. And from Brooke's tone of voice, neither could she. Kaylee had heard through the local grapevine that Brooke had left Turtle Cove about ten years ago, after the death of her grandmother, who had raised Brooke and a cousin. As Kaylee eyed the opulent gifts around her, she thought about how Brooke was in the midst of yet another life-changing event, the consequences of which could end up being even more catastrophic.

Kaylee's thoughts were interrupted when an authoritative voice, pitched at the perfect level to be heard over the buzz of the women's conversations, silenced the room.

"Gather over here, please. Over here, so I can give you instructions." Alicia Wellington-Simms, Brooke's wedding planner, commanded attention. While the other women were casually dressed, appropriate for the task they needed to accomplish, Alicia wore a tailored amethyst suit over a silk blouse a few shades lighter.

Interesting choice, considering Alicia herself chose amethyst as an accent color for the wedding over Brooke's more whimsical suggestions, Kaylee mused idly. Was it a coincidence, or had it been intentional? *Maybe she just likes amethyst. Either way, it's a good thing Brooke's not here to see it. That would probably hurt her.*

"We have a lot to do, ladies," Alicia said, her bright red lips stretched into a semblance of a smile. Kaylee thought it looked more like a sneer, but decided that was just because of her previous encounters with the wedding planner, who had come across as something of a bully in her dealings with the bride. "Each of these gifts needs to be carefully packaged. You'll find a card with the giver's name beside each gift." She picked up a card to show them, speaking slowly as though explaining the process to children. "Once you've closed the box, please tape the card on top. That way I can make sure all these items are returned to the proper persons."

She paused to look at the group, somehow reminding Kaylee of a general inspecting the troops. Perhaps she should salute. Tickled by the thought while simultaneously embarrassed by her silliness at such a sad time, Kaylee bit her lip to keep from giggling.

"That's our Alicia," Jessica whispered. "She loves to micromanage on a macro scale. Sometimes I think she just likes to hear herself talk."

Kaylee bit her lip even harder.

"Mrs. Roberts, do you have some packaging tip you'd like to share?" Alicia's haughty voice rang out. "No? Then please stop distracting Ms. Bleu. These instructions are important and will need to be followed to the letter." Without waiting for a response, Alicia gazed at her tablet, tapped the screen with perfectly manicured fingernails that exactly matched her suit, frowned as if in deep concentration, and then looked at her audience again. "This is a very sad day for all of us. One of our foremost citizens dead in the prime of his youth. His fiancée distraught with grief." Alicia gently dabbed beneath her heavily made-up eyes with her ring finger, then straightened as if rallying. "But it is only right we comply with what etiquette demands of us." She waved her hand toward the tables. "I have a roll of packaging tape for each of you. And one more thing, ladies. Don't break anything. That would be" . . . she paused and made eye contact with each of them . . . "unacceptable."

With that last warning, she disappeared into another room.

Kaylee and Jessica exchanged amused glances as they gathered boxes and tape.

"Could she be any bossier?" Kaylee said quietly enough so no one else could hear her.

"Alicia likes to be in charge. She always has, even when she was a child." Jessica led the way to a table and gasped. "Look at this." Her dark brown eyes, evidence of her Asian heritage, sparkled as she pointed to a substantial crystal vase. "Do you know what this is? A limited-edition Waterford," she continued before Kaylee could answer. "Isn't it lovely?"

"Beautiful," Kaylee agreed.

"And quite expensive." Jessica's gaze finally moved on from the vase and her mouth formed a perfect circle as she spotted something else. "And this. I know it's wrong to covet, but I'd love to have this blown-glass bowl. Do you think it's an original Chihuly?"

"If it is, I'm not touching it," Kaylee said. "I'll leave it in your capable hands."

"I'm not sure if Alicia agrees with your assessment. I keep expecting her to pop up and tell me my tape is on crooked." Jessica's expression turned sorrowful. "This isn't a time to be flippant is it? Poor Brooke."

"Have you talked to her?"

"Not for very long." Jessica wrapped the glass bowl in bubble wrap as she talked. "She didn't do it, you know. Sheriff Maddox treated her like a common criminal, taking her to his office and questioning her like that."

"I don't believe she did it either. The sheriff is only doing his job." Kaylee placed the ornate clock she had wrapped into a box and sealed it. Then she taped the card bearing the giver's name to the top of the box. Thankfully someone other than her would be responsible for shipping the gifts back to the senders. What a job that was going to be.

"I get it," Jessica said. "Brooke had the means and the opportunity and the motive. But I still don't believe she's guilty."

Kaylee gave Jessica a quizzical look. "What's her motive?"

"All that money."

"But they weren't married yet. Seems to me if Brooke was the murderer she would have waited until after the wedding to kill James, when she would actually inherit."

"Except he'd already taken out a multimillion-dollar life insurance policy naming her as the beneficiary."

"Is that true? I mean, do you know that for a fact?"

Jessica nodded. "Brooke told me herself. She's hired an attorney."

"Who?"

"Tyler Stevens."

"Didn't she date him?"

"They went out for a short while. In fact, he's how she met James. Apparently, James needed an interior designer to redo a room or something, and Tyler recommended the interior designer he was seeing, because she was new in town and hadn't quite gotten on her feet yet. He probably regretted that after she broke things off with him in favor of James."

"You know all the local gossip, don't you, Jess?" Kaylee teased.

"Whether or not I want to. You'd be surprised what people say over their coffee and dessert."

They wrapped and boxed a few more items before Jessica took a break to answer a phone call. Kaylee wandered toward the kitchen to get a glass of water, but her attention was caught by a large portrait displayed on an easel in a recessed nook of shuttered windows. Illuminated by overhead spotlights, the painting showed Brooke, wearing a white strapless dress and holding a large-brimmed hat. She stood in a vast field of lavender beneath a perfect blue sky. While Brooke was an attractive woman, the portrait was even more beautiful, catching her sweet spirit. It took a real artist to capture the subject's personality, not just their likeness.

Kaylee bent to see the signature.

R. Saunders.

She'd met local artist Rick Saunders a couple of times around town, but didn't know him well. His studio and gallery, located in a two-story house, was three or four blocks from The Flower Patch. The street had once been residential, but the homes had been transformed into shops and offices a decade or two ago.

Kaylee admired Rick's work and had thought about commissioning a portrait of Bear. It seemed like an indulgent expense though. A portrait of a dog?

Granted, this wasn't any dog. It was Bear.

Who was still at the vet clinic recovering from his bout with oleander poisoning.

If he had died, she'd always regret not having the portrait of her sweet little guy. She decided to talk to Rick as soon as possible.

Once all the gifts were packaged, Kaylee headed for the clinic to pick up Bear. She'd brought a different bow tie to replace the one he'd been wearing. When the vet assistant had tried to return the old one to her the previous night, she asked him to throw it away. She never wanted to see it again. She didn't need any more reminders of the terrible hours she thought she was going to lose her dog.

The bow tie she had now was tan with red and black fire hydrants, and it always gave Bear a jaunty look. He probably needed that now more than ever.

Her drive took her past Rick's studio and, on an impulse, Kaylee parked along the street. No time like the present to arrange for Bear's modeling debut.

She grinned at the thought, giddy with happiness that Bear would soon be back where he belonged. She'd slept fitfully last night without him snuggled against her legs. The cottage had seemed quite empty.

But tonight he'd be back home with her. She practically did a jig right there on the sidewalk at the thought.

Instead she bounded up the stairs to the broad porch. A decorative sign read *Saunders Portraits and Photography*, and the front door was flanked by huge gallery windows that showcased several large prints of Rick's original portraits.

Kaylee entered and stepped into an open gallery with a discreet counter tucked into a corner nook. Ceiling beams and thick wooden moldings indicated where the large space had once been divided into two smaller rooms.

In addition to several portraits, the gallery contained breathtaking seascapes. While waiting for someone to appear, Kaylee studied a painting of the lighthouse and gave an involuntary shiver. The widow's walk was a common feature of the tourist postcards sold around town. However, Kaylee didn't think she'd ever be able to look at it again without thinking of James.

The growing murmur of voices drew Kaylee toward an interior door that had been left slightly ajar.

She didn't mean to eavesdrop. She really didn't. But when James's name was mentioned, she couldn't help herself. The masculine voice was probably Rick Saunders. And Kaylee was pretty sure the feminine voice with its sophisticated and haughty pitch belonged to Alicia. Kaylee would have thought the wedding planner would still be at the keeper's cottage, preparing the gifts to be shipped back to those who had sent them.

"I'm not telling you anything you don't already know." Alicia's voice rose. "James's death, the death of the last remaining Stratford, is a great loss to our community. Sure, some people around here disliked him because he was such a shrewd businessman, but he kept the Stratford legacy alive."

Rick gave a noncommittal grunt.

"He and Brooke were so mismatched though. I had such grand ideas for this wedding, but she had to fight me on all of it. If he'd been marrying someone who actually suited him, it all would have gone a lot smoother."

"A man's art and his life—they have something in common."

"And what might that be?"

"So much of them depends on perception."

"What is that supposed to mean?" Alicia snapped.

"I don't think Brooke would agree with you about the two of them being mismatched. They may have seemed like completely different people, but they loved each other very much."

"Or perhaps that's the 'perception' they wanted everyone to have."

Kaylee, pretending to admire a nearby portrait of a young man who looked to be in his late teens crouching near railroad tracks, pictured Alicia making air quotes with her fingers on the word "perception."

"Believe me," Alicia continued, "I saw way too much of them together. He insisted on coming to all our consultations. Didn't he know the groom usually stays away?"

Rick gave a harsh laugh. "He did what he wanted. Even when we were kids. And he had the money to get away with it. He was a control freak. But I'm sure Brooke loved that he was taking an interest."

"I don't know why you're sticking up for him. Everyone knows how much the two of you hated each other."

"Hate is a strong word," Rick protested.

"What would you call it then?"

"We were lifelong rivals. That's all."

"I'd say it was more than that."

Alicia, followed closely by Rick, came through the door. Kaylee had been so involved in pretending not to eavesdrop that she hadn't realized the voices were getting closer. Alicia saw her, and her eyes narrowed.

Kaylee had been caught.

5

To hide her discomfort, Kaylee beamed a bright smile.

"Alicia. I didn't expect to see you here. I thought you were still at the lighthouse."

"I had a few errands," Alicia said coldly. "Besides, I had the utmost confidence that everyone there could follow my instructions. Did you find them difficult?"

"Can I help you with something?" Rick cut in before Kaylee could answer, his voice stilted, almost wary.

"I saw your portrait of Brooke," Kaylee said. "It's lovely."

Alicia huffed indignantly. "Yes, the loveliest vanity project a dead jerk's money can buy."

Rick cleared his throat and, as though Alicia hadn't spoken, said, "Thank you. James commissioned it. He had me do one of him a while back, and he wanted a matching one of his wife to display in their foyer, so everyone who came in would see them. He wanted that one to be displayed at the wedding to show off his money and his bride's beauty."

Kaylee smiled hesitantly. "I was wondering, would you consider—I mean, have you ever . . . Would you paint Bear?"

"Bear?"

"My dog."

Rick's expression changed from stoic to amused. "You mean that feisty weiner dog who rides around in your bicycle basket?"

"I didn't realize you'd noticed." Kaylee wasn't sure whether to be flattered or alarmed.

"Everyone around here has noticed. Small town, you know."

"True." Kaylee gave a hesitant smile. "Do you paint pets? Will you consider it?"

"Don't have to consider it." His smile broadened. "I'd be glad to."

"You cannot be serious," Alicia scoffed. "You are too talented an artist to indulge a . . . a whim."

"I think it'll be fun," Rick said. "The dog has a great face. I'd love to try to capture his personality."

Alicia made a strange snorting sound, but Kaylee ignored her. "That's wonderful," she said. "Thank you."

"The first thing I'll need to do is take a few photographs. Today is kind of crazy, so would it be okay if I call you later to set up an appointment time?"

"Absolutely." Kaylee grinned. "Bear's first photo shoot. How exciting. Thank you so much."

"I heard Bear drank some of the tea that killed James," Alicia said, almost in an offhanded way as she inspected her perfect nails.

If she had meant to douse Kaylee's exuberant spirit with her cold words, she succeeded.

"He did," Kaylee said. "But he's going to be okay. I'm picking him up from the vet as soon as I leave here."

"How nice." Alicia dug in her bag for a ring of keys, then stretched her bright red lips into a cheerless smile. "I must return to the lighthouse to see about the last of the gifts."

"They're all boxed and labeled," Kaylee said.

"I'm sure Brooke appreciates everything you and your friends are doing for her during this horrible time."

"We're glad to help."

"You'll be available on Monday, won't you? So we can talk about the wedding flowers? We'll need to come to some arrangement."

"Right," Kaylee said slowly. With her mind consumed by James's murder and Bear's poisoning, she hadn't given much thought to all the wedding flowers stored in her coolers. What did other florists do when the bridegroom was murdered the day before the wedding?

Tension chilled the atmosphere, and Kaylee realized that even though Alicia had said she was leaving, she hadn't taken even one step toward the door. Obviously she was waiting for Kaylee to leave.

She handed Rick her business card. "Call anytime," she said. "If I'm not there, just leave a message."

"I'll do that. Or maybe I'll drop by."

"That would be fine too." She nodded to Alicia and left the gallery. Once outside, she exhaled the pent-up tension from her body. What was it about Rick and Alicia's conversation that had put her on edge? Probably nothing more than nerves and worries. Everything had been tense the last few days.

It was definitely time to get Bear and take him home. As she crossed the street to her car, her cell rang.

"Hi, Jess. What's up?" she asked.

"Have you heard the latest?" Jessica sounded on the verge of hysteria. "Brooke's been taken to the police station again."

"Why?"

"They found a plant inside her garage. An oleander."

Kaylee cuddled the little dachshund in her arms and kissed the top of his rounded head. "How are you, Bear" she murmured. "All better now?"

"He's doing remarkably well," Dr. Melody said. "He must not have ingested too much of the tea. And you got him here so quickly we were able to start treatment almost immediately."

"Thanks to Nick Durham," Kaylee said.

"I'd say he helped to save Bear's life."

"So did you." Kaylee made a mental note to send a bouquet to the vet. "I can't thank you enough."

"I'm glad we're celebrating a success." The doctor stroked Bear's ear. "No more drinking things you shouldn't, little man."

Bear gave a tiny bark as if to say he absolutely wouldn't, and Kaylee and Dr. Melody laughed. After receiving final instructions, Kaylee was about to leave when Dr. Melody stopped her.

"Is it true Brooke's been arrested?" she asked.

"I'm not sure," Kaylee said. She had promised the sheriff she wouldn't share her own theory that Brooke was the intended victim, not the murderer. There was no need to add grist to the gossip mill. "She may have been taken in for questioning, but I doubt they have enough evidence to charge her."

"I suppose that's not unusual. Don't the police always suspect the significant other first?"

"It's a place to start."

Dr. Melody made a notation on Bear's chart, then scratched his head fondly. "When she was a teenager, Brooke volunteered at the local animal shelter one summer when I was doing an internship. Don't tell anybody, but I was always partial to the dogs."

"Your secret is safe with me. I like dogs best too."

"Not Brooke, though. She loved the kittens. Even raised a couple of motherless litters. Strange, isn't it?"

"What's that?"

"Not long ago, someone dropped off a kitten he'd found near the Turtleback Mountain Preserve. The poor little baby couldn't have been more than a few days old. I asked Brooke if she wanted to mother it."

"What did she say?"

"That's what was so strange. She said she was allergic to cats."

"Allergic?"

"I suppose it's something she could have developed as an adult. And maybe she just didn't want to take on the responsibility with the wedding and all. But I wish she'd just said no rather than make up an excuse."

"I think Brooke has a hard time saying no. It seems she wants to get along with everyone, to fit in."

"She was always like that," Dr. Melody said. "A far cry from James Stratford. He was never one to shy away from saying whatever was on his mind."

"You didn't like him?"

"We moved in different circles, so I didn't know him very well. But I've been at enough town hall meetings to know James wasn't shy." She handed Bear's discharge papers to Kaylee. "Be sure Bear takes it easy for the next couple of days."

"I will. Thanks again for everything."

With Bear in her arms, Kaylee left the vet's office and headed toward her red Ford Escape. Parked next to it was a shiny black pickup. Reese Holt, Turtle Cove's most sought-after handyman, leaned against the cab, eyes glued to his phone.

James Stratford might have been Orcas Island's most eligible bachelor because of his millions, but Reese was a close second thanks to his rugged good looks and easygoing manner. Plus, he was a handyman extraordinaire, which had endeared him to Bea and now Kaylee, who had called him more than once to fix something at Wildflower Cottage.

A gusty breeze played with Reese's sandy brown hair. As usual, he wore a plaid flannel shirt over a blue T-shirt and jeans. He looked up, and his lips parted into a disarming smile. Kaylee's heart beat a little faster. But she firmly told herself it was because she was so relieved that Bear was okay.

"Hey there," Reese said as she drew nearer. "What's this I hear about Bear being poisoned?"

"It's true," Kaylee said. "But he's fine now, thanks to Dr. Melody."

"She's the best." Reese cleared his throat. "I heard you were the one who found James. I mean after he died."

"I did." Kaylee looked down and studied Bear's fur. "He was on the lighthouse widow's walk."

"I'm sorry it was you, Kaylee. Are you doing okay?"

Kaylee flashed a small, brief smile at him as she realized he was the first person to ask her that question. Everyone else asked about Bear or about Brooke. It was nice to know someone cared about how all this affected her.

"I'm okay," she said. "Though it was a shock to see him like that."

Shocking enough she'd hardly slept the night before, in fact. Bear's absence wasn't the only reason for her restlessness. Her troubling dreams, disturbing in their vivid yet unconnected imagery, had her wishing for time to take an afternoon nap.

"I can't even imagine." Reese let a somber moment pass, but then his charming grin took over his face again. "Seems like everyone in town is at loose ends this evening since the wedding has been canceled. How about meeting me at the diner for a good old-fashioned burger? I'll buy."

"Sounds fun, but I can't." After Jessica's frantic phone call, Kaylee's plans for a quiet evening had turned into an impromptu Petal Pushers gathering. "The Petals are coming over tonight. This has been stressful on all of us, and we just wanted to be together."

Kaylee squeezed Bear a little tighter, trying to gather her thoughts. Apparently she was more on edge than she realized. But who wouldn't be? She'd come so close to losing her sweet dog. Even worse, she'd stumbled on a dead body. Someone in her beloved Turtle Cove was a murderer. Someone who hated James enough to kill him. Or hated Brooke enough that James had been caught in a deadly cross fire.

Despite Sheriff Maddox's "misdirection" theory, Kaylee couldn't believe James had been killed by his fiancée. But she also had no idea who had murdered him.

"You gals don't fool me," Reese said. "I bet you'll spend all evening trying to figure out what happened to James. And why."

"You're probably not wrong. It seems that's all anybody wants to talk about around here."

"For better or worse." Reese regarded her carefully. "Are you sure you're okay?"

"It's been a long couple of days, that's for sure." Kaylee shifted Bear's weight in her arms. Amazing how heavy the little guy could get. "Anyway, I ought to get Bear home. He still has some recovering to do."

"If you need anything, you've got my number."

"Thanks. I'll give you a call. That is, if I need anything."

Reese opened the back door of Kaylee's SUV for her, and she set Bear in the carrier she had on the backseat. Usually he rode in the passenger seat up front, but she knew he would appreciate the blanket-lined carrier until he felt like his old self again.

After saying goodbye to Reese, Kaylee sank into the driver's seat. Though she needed to get home and prepare for the Petal Pushers, she closed her eyes as weariness settled around her. Reese was probably right. They'd talk about the murder and about Brooke. But would they solve the mystery?

Could they?

6

The oven timer dinged and Kaylee pulled a steamy casserole dish from the oven.

"Smells good," DeeDee said as she arranged deli sandwiches on a tray. "What is it?"

"Sour cream, cream cheese, bacon bits, shredded cheese, and diced jalapenos." Kaylee set the hot dish on a trivet in the middle of the island. "I found the recipe online. It was quick and easy."

"I love the Internet." Mary dipped a cracker in the dip, then blew on it before she popped it in her mouth. Her blue eyes sparkled behind her stylish frames. "Yum. I love this too. And it would probably be really easy to change it up if you're going for a different flavor."

Jessica reached for her own cracker. "That's the best kind of recipe. Just be sure to leave room for dessert."

"What did you bring?" Mary asked.

"A tray of assorted chocolate delights intended for last night's rehearsal dinner. Is it morbid I brought them?"

"No need for them to go to waste," Mary said, consoling Jessica with a quick hug. "I don't even know why I bother trying to diet. With you as a friend, Jess, I'm doomed to carrying around these extra pounds the rest of my life."

Kaylee and DeeDee exchanged amused glances. Mary might be the grandmother of the group, but she was as physically fit as any of them. Maybe Kaylee should take up tai chi too. Mary had often asked her to come along to the weekly class.

Jessica raised an eyebrow. "What extra pounds? I don't think your body even knows how to produce them."

"I'm not kidding," Mary protested. "I gain five pounds just by walking into the bakery. All those delicious aromas."

A delighted smile brightened Jessica's features, but there was still a hint of sadness and worry behind it. It wasn't hard for Kaylee to guess what was bothering her. Brooke's suspected involvement in James's murder had affected each of them to some degree, but Jessica most of all. Her daughter, Mila, had been friends with Brooke and her cousin before the two girls moved away. Brooke was like another daughter to Jessica.

DeeDee handed Jessica a glass of iced tea. "We're all sorry about Brooke. Any updates?"

"I spent most of the afternoon with her," Jessica said. "Let's serve ourselves and then we can talk."

Within a few minutes, the women were seated around the island with chicken salad croissants, fresh veggies, and DeeDee's infamous pasta salad.

"Saturday night with the ladies," Mary said, raising her glass. "One of my favorite pastimes."

"Mine too," Kaylee said. "Though I always feel a little guilty taking you all from your husbands on what should be a date night."

"It's not a problem for Jess and me," Mary said. "Without a wedding to go to, our husbands decided to spend the evening together. Tax season, you know."

"They're working late hours?" Kaylee asked.

"The life of an accountant," Jessica said. "Luke's popular this time of year. And Herb is one of his favorite clients. Don't feel sorry for me, though. We plan an annual getaway the first weekend of May. This year we're thinking of British Columbia. That's where we went on our honeymoon." Her flash of cheerfulness faded. "Poor Brooke. She and James had such grand honeymoon plans. A week in New York City and another in Savannah. She was so excited. She'd never been that far east before."

"It does sound fun, but your trip sounds wonderful too." Kaylee tried to sound encouraging, both to help Jess feel better and to steer the subject away from the day's tragedy. "What is Andy up to this evening?" she asked DeeDee.

"With the wedding canceled, he and our girls went to Seattle to visit his parents for the weekend. I'm glad we planned this little get-together. Otherwise, I'd be home watching TV."

"I wish Brooke had come," Jessica said. "I don't even want to imagine how lonely she must feel. But she insisted she wanted to be alone."

"She's had a rough day," Mary said. "How long was she with the sheriff?"

"Hours." Jessica speared pasta with her fork more viciously than she needed to. "All the evidence is circumstantial, but it's strong. I think if Sheriff Maddox finds out anything else that points to her as being the—" Jessica stopped, unable to bring herself to say the horrible word.

"Aren't there *any* other suspects?" Kaylee turned toward Mary. As a retired police dispatcher, she had several law enforcement contacts. "Have you heard anything?"

Mary shook her head. "Nothing. Eddie is staying close-lipped about this one."

"Luke said James might be involved in a shady business deal." Jessica covered her mouth with her hand. "I don't think I was supposed to tell anyone that."

"Your secret is safe with us," Mary said. "I imagine James has had business troubles before though. I can't imagine anyone would kill him over something like that."

"People have killed over business dealings before. Perhaps he cheated someone," DeeDee suggested. "And that person wanted revenge."

"I always heard he was a shrewd businessman, but a fair one," Mary argued.

"Or maybe he's leading a double life!" Jessica's brown eyes lit up as she slapped a hand on the table. Always one for a conspiracy theory, the spunky baker could make up the most elaborate story from the smallest details. "And his current wife found out about his engagement. She confronted him, but he told her he didn't care what she said or did. They argued. He stormed out. She followed him and—" Jessica's eyes widened and her facial muscles tensed. "Hell hath no fury like a woman scorned."

"Oh, Jess." Mary gave a good-natured laugh. "Where would James hide another family?"

"Anywhere he wanted. He's got money," Jessica said, as if that decided the argument. "Or he had it anyway. People with money can do all kinds of things the rest of us can't."

After church the next day, Kaylee drove to the lighthouse to check on the new shrubs that had been planted a couple of days earlier. The wedding had been called off, but that was no reason not to tend to the bushes. Assuming they survived, at least something good could come of the never-to-be nuptials.

She felt as though she wore a blanket of melancholy, and she thought that doing something with her hands might help keep it at bay. She'd had another restless night, full of strange dreams that faded when she awoke only to return when she drifted off to sleep again.

In the dreams, Brooke stood on the opposite end of an oleander meadow. As she sank into a lake of honey, she begged Kaylee to save her. Kaylee tried running toward her, but the oleander leaves and stems encircled her legs. Bees buzzed around the fragrant flowers and in front of Kaylee's eyes—huge bees with stingers like stilettos. Despite all her efforts, Kaylee was powerless.

She might never get a good night's sleep again if she didn't do something to solve this mystery and clear Brooke's name. She couldn't say how she knew, but her intuition told her that Brooke had not killed James. She had loved him, adored him, and she was a good person. Never would she have done anything so vile, even to someone she didn't love.

Unfortunately, this certainty left her with no ideas, no leads about who the murderer could be.

After she parked, Kaylee removed her dressy heels and slipped on a pair of canvas shoes she kept in the SUV for times like this. The grounds seemed deserted, and a finger of fear traced up Kaylee's spine. She shivered in the strong breeze gusting from the ocean and put on the jacket she also kept in the vehicle. The weather was warm enough that she usually didn't need it, but near the ocean, there was no way to predict how the air would feel. Hands in her pockets, she crossed the grounds to the lighthouse.

She circled the building, inspecting the shrubs she had planted on Friday. Satisfied that the pink-bloomed red currant bushes were thriving despite being inopportunely uprooted, Kaylee started toward her car, then stopped. She gazed up at the widow's walk. *Maybe I can think more clearly up there, where it all happened.*

Once inside the keeper's cottage, she peered up the staircase well, heaved a large sigh, and began the long climb to the top. Kaylee both dreaded and felt compelled to see again the stain of the oleander-poisoned tea where James had died, even though she knew she would vividly remember finding his body, hand outstretched toward the spilled silver travel mug.

As she mounted the steps, she asked herself why someone had poisoned the honey. No clear answer came, only emotions and images: her panicked fear when Bear convulsed in her arms, Brooke's pale features frozen in shock, and Jessica's distress that one of her daughters' childhood friends was suspected of murder.

When Kaylee reached the widow's walk, she paused by the railing and gazed toward the distant horizon. Water, sky, and land intersected in wild, indistinct boundaries. The sea air—so fresh and clean and pure—chilled her face and filled her lungs.

In generations past, numerous women had stood on this walk, their eyes glued to the horizon as they waited for the first glimpse of a white sail against the azure sky. Their hearts, full of longing for the return of their menfolk, must have practically burst when the ships appeared.

Kaylee pressed her palms against the railing and mentally shook herself back to present day. Thankfully she wasn't standing here in hopes of seeing an overdue ship sailing into the harbor. Such thoughts sounded romantic in historical novels, but she appreciated the life she had now too much to ever want to trade places with one of those forlorn, waiting women.

Done with her daydreaming, she followed the widow's walk around the corner of the lighthouse to where yellow crime tape flapped in the wind. It wasn't her place to remove the tape, but she wished she could yank it from the railing. Granted, its removal wouldn't change what happened here.

The poisoned tea had stained the wood. Perhaps the frequent rains would eventually cleanse the boards, but how long would that take? However long it was, she knew it would take longer to cleanse Brooke's heart of grief.

James had died a sickening death. Despite Kaylee's every hope to the contrary, his bride was the only one who seemed to have a motive, the means, and the opportunity to poison him.

It just can't be Brooke.

Kaylee sighed heavily. Coming here had been futile, a complete waste of time. There were no answers, only sad reminders. In frustration, she tugged on the fluttering tape, but whoever had tied it to the railing must be a pro with knots. It held firm.

She returned to the entrance to the stairway, then paused to look out over the horizon one more time. It might be a long time before she climbed those steps again. Maybe she should take a couple of photos before she left. As she reached into her pocket for her phone, she noticed movement on the beach. A man and a woman were jogging along the shore.

Just like . . . yes, the day James died. She had stood in this very spot, looking out over the beach. A jogger had been there that day too. Not a jogger. A runner. Someone had been running away from the lighthouse.

Kaylee's mind whirled with self-recrimination and also hope. She shouldn't have forgotten such an important detail as actually witnessing someone running from the scene of the crime. Being worried about Bear wasn't an excuse for that kind of neglect, especially not for someone with her experience working with law enforcement.

But there wasn't anything she could do about that now except to admit her mistake and tell Sheriff Maddox what she had seen. The presence of another person might be helpful to Brooke's defense. After all, she couldn't have been running along the beach that day because she'd been with Jessica.

Kaylee played out a scenario in her mind, trying to shift the guilt to this mysterious person. But it did no good. Her initial euphoria faded as she mentally reviewed the case's evidence.

James had died from drinking poisoned tea. Even if someone else had been with him on the widow's walk, that person probably hadn't poisoned the honey in the tea. If only James had died from something else—like a knife wound or a bump on the head—then the mystery runner would take Brooke's place as the number one suspect.

The more Kaylee thought about what she had seen that morning, the more she was convinced the runner wasn't jogging for exercise but to get away.

Or was she grasping at straws because she wanted to prove Brooke was innocent?

Kaylee descended the stairs then crossed the lighthouse grounds to the beach. Peering around for any clues, she followed the route the runner had taken that dreadful morning.

She walked slowly, though she had small hope of finding anything useful. More than forty-eight hours had passed since James's death. The daily tides washed away footprints, and the runner certainly hadn't taken the time to write a message in the sand.

Despite her discouragement—or perhaps because of her guilt for not remembering the runner sooner—Kaylee plodded along the path leading from the beach through the scrub. She kicked at a soda can and watched it tumble along the ground. Anyone could have dropped the can anytime, though why people littered . . . *no, focus, Kaylee.*

She took a few more steps then a slight flutter caught her eye. She bent down and stared at the white-edged paper. No, not paper. A photograph. A torn photograph. Her heart rate quickened as she gingerly picked up the photo by its corner. It had been torn in half, and she scanned the surrounding area for its mate.

"There you are," she said, pleased with her discovery. Handling both halves by their corners, she placed them next to each other. The photograph showed two young girls, perhaps eleven or twelve, with their arms around each other's shoulders. They stood in front of the lighthouse, both of them smiling, both of them practically bursting with youthful energy.

And both of them looking amazingly alike. Not identical, but close enough to be sisters.

"Who are you?" Kaylee said quietly. She stared at the images, then focused on one of the girls. "It's got to be. It's Brooke."

But how did the photo get here? And why had it been torn in half?

The photograph didn't look too damaged by weather, so Kaylee didn't think it had been out there for any length of time. What if the mystery runner had torn the photo and thrown it on the ground? That was possible. A breeze could have blown it beneath the grasses where it had been protected.

All that was plausible, but so were a thousand other explanations. Even so, Kaylee would treat the ripped photograph as a clue. She pulled two specimen bags from her jacket pocket—as a forensic botanist, she always carried a few with her—and placed one half of the photograph in each bag.

Now she needed to decide what to do with them.

She should probably show them to Sheriff Maddox. But what if he thought she was making up a flimsy excuse for casting blame on someone other than Brooke? Perhaps the torn photograph was additional proof that the murderer was after Brooke instead of James, that James's death had been a mistake.

Kaylee wasn't sure what to think. She returned to her SUV and headed north to Turtle Cove. Her initial impulse was to go home to Wildflower Cottage, which was on the other side of town. On a whim, she decided to go to the Pacific Street Diner instead. A cup of coffee would be nice, and since Jessica's coffee shop was closed on Sundays, the diner was the next best option.

Once settled in a booth, Kaylee ordered coffee and a piece of coconut cream pie, then took her planner from her bag. She needed to do something to get her mind off the murder case. This was a good time to review the coming week. She opened the agenda to

Monday's page and tried not to groan as she wrote Alicia's name in the appointment section. The wedding planner hadn't specified a time but Kaylee expected Alicia would drop by in the morning. That was her preferred time for any consultation meetings.

Kaylee absentmindedly doodled in the space near Alicia's name. She had no idea what to do in a situation like this—or what Alicia might be expecting. Per the shop's policy, established when Bea had opened its doors, James had already made payment in full. But the idea of profiting from the unused wedding flowers made Kaylee sick to her stomach.

Mary had mentioned last night that The Flower Patch had already received several orders for James's funeral, but there was no way Kaylee could bring herself to recycle the unused wedding flowers into funeral flowers for the groom. She thought about calling Bea for advice, but then she remembered that her grandmother was still on her cruise, far from civilization.

"Hi, Kaylee."

She looked up, startled to see Reese standing beside her booth. Instead of his typical handyman attire, he wore khakis and a blue pullover.

"Hey, there."

"Mind if I join you?"

"Not at all."

"You sure? You look preoccupied."

"Just thinking about tomorrow."

He lowered himself into the booth, a thoughtful expression on his face. "I suppose you'll be busy."

"Funerals are the only thing I don't like about owning a flower shop," she said, surprising even herself with her admission. She often found herself saying things to Reese that she wouldn't say to anyone else. Something about him seemed to inspire confidences.

"Your grandmother told me the same thing once."

"She did?"

"Yeah." Reese paused while the waitress set Kaylee's pie in front of her. "Looks good. Think I'll have one too."

"With coffee?" asked the waitress.

"Sure."

After the waitress left, Reese smiled at Kaylee. "Your grandmother is so proud of you."

"How do you know?"

"We talk sometimes."

"You do? What about?"

"Most recently, about my annual spruce-up of The Flower Patch and Wildflower Cottage."

"I don't know anything about that."

"I have a list." He tapped his head. "Up here. I've been doing it for years . . . just making sure everything is shipshape."

"Are you trying to drum up business?" Kaylee teased.

"Already have the business. It's her present to you. We only need to decide on a date." He gestured toward the open planner. "Got any free time in that thing?"

"Why didn't Grandma say anything to me about this?"

Reese shrugged. "All I know is she told me to talk to you about it."

Kaylee took a bite of her pie so she wouldn't have to respond. She knew exactly what her grandmother was up to—a little matchmaking. Kaylee appreciated the gesture, and she appreciated the present. But she didn't need anyone's help finding a boyfriend. And she especially didn't want Reese to suspect her grandmother's ulterior motive. The best way to handle this was to be as businesslike as possible. That meant she couldn't scowl at her pie no matter how much she wanted to.

"I don't need to be there, do I?" she asked, forcefully keeping her expression pleasant. "At the cottage, I mean."

"Nope. Like I said, I've been doing this for years. I know all the quirks of the mansion and the cottage."

"Then any day will be fine. Whatever works for your schedule."

"I'm free next week."

Kaylee flipped a page in her planner and they decided on a day and time.

"How was your evening with the Petal Pushers?" Reese asked after Kaylee had finished writing his name in her planner. "Was I right about the hot topic of the night?"

"No surprise there. James and Brooke are on everyone's mind." Kaylee picked up her fork and toyed with her pie. "It's so awful what happened. Jess asked Brooke to come over, but she said she wanted to stay home. I guess she wanted to be alone."

"I don't think so."

"Why not?"

"Her neighbor across the street had an emergency plumbing situation. Since I was there, I thought I'd check on her, see how she was holding up. But she wasn't home."

"That's odd," Kaylee said, more to herself than to Reese. "I wonder where she was." *And why Brooke lied to Jessica.*

7

After leaving the diner, Kaylee drove to Brooke's home and parked on the street. This was one of Turtle Cove's older neighborhoods, and the homes were modest but mostly well-maintained with small, tidy lawns. A few overgrown shrubs and untamed trees gave the street a welcoming, hospitable atmosphere.

The blinds were closed at Brooke's home—a beige bungalow with forest-green shutters—but her car was in the driveway. She had insisted on staying in the house she'd rented when she first returned to town until after the wedding.

Kaylee stepped out of her car and quietly shut her door. At least the reporters were no longer around. They were probably spending Sunday afternoon at home with their families. That's where Kaylee should be—at home, minding her own business and spending time with her dog.

But she was too involved with this case to put it out of her mind.

Maybe if she hadn't found James's body. Maybe if Bear hadn't gotten sick. Maybe if she hadn't seen the mystery runner on the beach or found the photograph. All kinds of maybes ran through her mind.

Added together, though, they were a heavy burden. She had to find out the identity of the mystery runner. She had to help Brooke find the answers that would keep her out of prison.

Gathering all her courage, Kaylee strode to the front door and rang the bell. A moment later, Brooke slowly opened the door and looked suspiciously beyond Kaylee. Dark circles rimmed her eyes, and her complexion appeared wan.

"Are you alone?"

"Yes."

She barely opened the door wide enough for Kaylee to squeeze in, closed it firmly, and then turned the lock and the dead bolt.

"Brooke, are you all right?"

"Of course I'm not all right."

"That's not how I meant it."

Brooke waved her hand in an apologetic gesture. "I know you didn't. Please. Come in. Sit down."

Kaylee fumbled for words, finally settling on the tired cliché. "I'm truly sorry for what happened."

"Do you think I killed him?"

Though taken aback by the directness of the question, Kaylee didn't hesitate to answer. "No, I don't."

"A lot of people around here do."

"That's because they don't know you."

Brooke gave Kaylee a cynical look. "You don't really know me either."

"True. But I know you well enough to know you could never do something like that."

"It's nice to know not everyone believes I'm a monster." Brooke plopped on the sofa and wrapped her arms around her legs. "If you came to look at the oleander plant found in my garage, you're too late. The sheriff took it."

Kaylee sat on the other end of the sofa. "Do you have any idea how it got there?"

"I never saw it before." Brooke pressed her fingers against her temples. "But I'm not sure Sheriff Maddox believes me."

"He's only doing his job."

Brooke grunted her disagreement, then apparently regretted doing so. She forced a smile and the tone of her voice lightened. "I've forgotten my manners. Would you like something to drink?"

"No thank you. I just stopped by to ask you about something."

"More incriminating evidence in my garage that I know nothing about?"

"Something I found."

Brooke shifted, leaning against the arm of the sofa, and pulled her legs beneath her. "A clue to James's killer?"

"That morning, I saw someone running on the beach. In all the confusion, I forgot about it." Kaylee told Brooke about visiting the lighthouse and her own beach excursion, then handed her the two specimen bags. "I found these under a bush."

Brooke placed the two halves of the photograph as close together as she could. Her lips parted in a sad smile. "I remember this day. We'd been sailing. Such a warm and beautiful summer day."

"The two of you look so much alike."

"She's my cousin. Beth." Her voice turned pensive. "Our moms were twins."

"Will Beth be at the funeral?" Kaylee asked gently. "I'd love to meet her."

Brooke didn't answer right away. "She can't come," she finally said. She stood abruptly. "You know, I don't think I've ever seen this photograph before."

"It's not yours?"

"No. Thanks for giving it to me."

"You can't keep it."

"Why not?"

"It might be evidence."

"Evidence of what?"

Kaylee bit her lip. "I don't know, Brooke. Maybe of nothing. But don't you think it's odd? A photograph you've never seen is torn apart and left on the beach. I find it only a couple of days after—" She couldn't bring herself to finish the sentence.

"I suppose," Brooke said doubtfully. Tears welled in her eyes. "Kaylee, I don't know what to think. I only know I didn't poison James. I wouldn't have."

"I know." Kaylee stood and gently took the specimen bags from Brooke's clenched fingers. "I think I should show these to Sheriff Maddox. Maybe when he hears my story, he'll stop thinking of you as the primary suspect."

"Do you really think so?"

"I don't know. But it's worth a try, isn't it?"

"I guess. Thank you, Kaylee."

Kaylee nodded and said goodbye. Once she was back in her car, she drove north to Wildflower Cottage. It had been a long day, and she needed to get home to check on Bear. After her meeting with Alicia tomorrow, she'd make the drive to the sheriff's office in Eastsound. Until then, she'd enjoy a quiet evening at home with Bear. Hopefully, she could put everything to do with Brooke and James out of her mind for at least a little while. Maybe she'd even get a good night's sleep for once.

Later that evening, after a light supper of leftover chicken salad, Kaylee carried Bear up the steep stairs to the cottage's attic. The old photograph she'd found on the shore had her thinking about all the photos her grandmother had left behind. Kaylee meant to take her role as keeper of the family history seriously.

Even though she didn't have children of her own, she had two lovely and lively nieces, seven-year-old Isabella and five-year-old Mattie. Kaylee's brother, Kyle, and his family lived almost as far away from Kaylee as possible while staying in the continental US. Shortly after his marriage, he and his wife, Linda, moved to the Gulf coast of western Florida for their jobs. Kaylee's parents now lived there too, so they could be close to their grandchildren.

Since her nieces seldom visited Orcas Island, Kaylee decided to create photo albums for each of them that showcased their heritage. The albums would be Kaylee's contribution to the family legacy and, hopefully, a treasured memento for the girls.

Kaylee removed the dustcover from a wobbly walnut dresser and took two old family albums from the bottom drawer. For several minutes, she perused the older album, a collection of sepia-toned and black-and-white photographs tucked into mounted corners on thick rectangular paper and bound between two hard covers. She smiled at the faded images of Grandma and Grandpa as children, teenagers, and eventually young adults. Kaylee supposed Grandma must have compiled the album, since it contained photographs of both sides of the family, including the great-grandparents Kaylee had never known.

Some of the people were strangers. Bea had written their names on the backs of some of the photographs, but others were blank. Perhaps someone at the historical society could identify the mystery people, or she could put them on display at the flower shop. People might enjoy coming in to see if they recognized anyone from the old photos. Or what if she compiled them into some type of book along with other old photos from other island residents? Maybe she could put together a history of Orcas Island or something like that.

Cool it, Kaylee.

Didn't she already have enough to do?

Sure she did. But the idea persisted, and she felt the tug on her heartstrings that told her this was a project she wanted to pursue. Grandma and Grandpa had been notable and respected citizens of the community. Kaylee wanted to honor them and others who had helped create such a fine place for Turtle Cove's residents.

Motivated, Kaylee set to her task. Once she finished with the first album, she retrieved a stack of loose photographs from the drawer. The best way to sort these, she decided, was to make three piles: one of photos to have duplicated for her nieces, one of photos she wanted to keep, and one for the historical society or anyone else who might want them.

Five minutes later, there weren't many photos left in the giveaway pile.

She got busy with another stack but was interrupted by the chiming of her cell phone. DeeDee's name and image appeared on the screen.

"Hi," Kaylee said. "What's up?"

"Did you hear the news?" DeeDee's voice sounded glum.

Kaylee fought a sudden onset of panic. What else could have gone wrong?

"What news?" she asked.

"Brooke's been arrested. Officially."

Kaylee's stomach turned to lead. "I just talked to her a couple of hours ago. What happened?"

"She left the island." DeeDee sighed heavily. "The authorities apprehended her when the ferry docked on the mainland."

"She could have had errands to do," Kaylee said, though she knew she was grasping at straws even as the words left her mouth. "Or maybe she just needed to get away from this mess for a little while."

"Except that Sheriff Maddox had told her to stay put. She wasn't allowed to leave."

"Where is she now?"

"They're keeping her overnight on the mainland. From what I understand, the sheriff will take the first ferry in the morning then bring her back."

"She isn't guilty."

"Maybe not," DeeDee said. "But she hasn't helped herself any by trying to leave."

Kaylee didn't know what to say, and for a moment the line was silent.

"I just can't imagine what she was thinking," DeeDee continued. "She had to know this would make her look even guiltier. I wish I could ask her why."

"Maybe it's my fault," Kaylee said.

"Your fault? What did you do?"

"I found a photograph on the beach this afternoon."

"What photograph?"

"It was a picture of Brooke and her cousin when they were children," Kaylee said. "I showed it to her but she said she'd never seen it before."

"I don't see how that would make her want to get out of Dodge."

"Me either." Kaylee's thoughts once again seemed to be going in circles. Nothing about this made any sense. But what else could have happened to cause Brooke to try to leave? Whether or not Kaylee was to blame, she felt responsible. "I should have called the sheriff right after I talked to Brooke. But I didn't think another day would make any difference. Especially since today is Sunday."

"I don't see how a photograph of Brooke as a child has anything to do with James's murder," DeeDee said. "I've been thinking of all the mysteries I've read over the years, and that seems like a far-fetched clue to me."

"But sometimes the strangest clues turn out to be the most important ones."

"I suppose," DeeDee said. "Please don't worry about it anymore tonight, Kaylee. You can talk to the sheriff in the morning. There's nothing that can be done for Brooke until then."

The two women chatted for a few more minutes before Kaylee ended the call.

"What do you think, Bear?" she asked as she picked up the dachshund. "Shall we call it a day and hope we find some answers tomorrow?"

She went downstairs and released Bear into the yard one more time before going to bed. She gazed at the view in the velvety darkness. Above the mountain range, the stars shone clear and bright in the night sky, tiny pinpricks of light reaching from the edges of the universe. How very sad that Brooke couldn't see them.

Kaylee couldn't bear to imagine what Brooke must be going through. How awful to have been stopped, perhaps even handcuffed, as she got off the ferry.

"Why did you do it, Brooke?" Kaylee whispered to the night sky. "Why did you run?"

At The Flower Patch the next morning, Kaylee consulted her Edgars/Stratford wedding file, running her finger down the long list of bouquets, boutonnieres, centerpieces, and other floral arrangements requested for the wedding. It had been her largest order since she took over the shop from Bea, and she and Mary had worked long hours to ensure the flowers were perfect. Bear, mostly recovered from his ordeal but still sticking close to her, sat at her feet. Today his bow tie was navy blue sprinkled with white anchors.

Alicia fidgeted nearby, her demeanor clearly indicating her impatience. Her long nails, a chic brown today, tapped on the table as she studied an open document on her electronic tablet. Kaylee supposed she was consulting her own list.

"Everything was completed except for the bridal bouquets," Kaylee said. "We already have the flowers, but Mary and I were going to put them together Saturday morning. Brooke had a special lace handkerchief she wanted to add to the bouquet. It belonged to her grandmother."

"Then you won't mind if I deduct their cost from the invoice," Alicia said coolly. She stared at Kaylee over the top of a pair of stylish half-rim glasses. "Certainly you don't want to take advantage of Brooke in her time of grief."

Kaylee ignored the offensive insinuation and glanced at Mary, whose stoic expression was little help. "I don't know the protocol in a situation like this," she admitted.

"I'm sure you can use the flowers another way." Alicia glanced at the various arrangements displayed on the table. "It's a shame, though. This gorgeous wedding, all the planning I did, and now it's not to be. Your designs are quite nice. Much better than I dared hope."

"Excuse me," Mary said, a slight edge to her voice. Bear heard it and whined softly.

Kaylee caught Mary's gaze and shook her head. As much as she appreciated her friend's loyalty, she'd dealt with her share of people at the university who, like Alicia, seemed to enjoy baiting their peers with backhanded compliments and snide remarks. She could handle Alicia Wellington-Simms.

At first, Kaylee had been honored when Brooke insisted on choosing The Flower Patch for her flowers instead of one of the snooty flower shops on the mainland Alicia had wanted her to use. Certainly the prestige of providing flowers for James Stratford's wedding was good for business—not to mention the profit. But working with Alicia had been a headache from day one.

"I didn't mean to imply you couldn't do it," Alicia said smoothly, her bright red lips stretched into a plastic smile. "Only I had strongly suggested that Brooke choose Carringtons out of Olympia. They did all the flowers for the wedding of the governor's daughter last fall." Alicia clasped her hands together, gazed toward the ceiling with a look of rapture, and gave a dreamy sigh. "Every aspect of that wedding was absolutely exquisite."

She turned back to Kaylee and Mary. "And of course, James could afford the best. But Brooke wanted you. The local flower shop."

"I suppose she preferred working with friends instead of strangers," Mary said tightly.

The front door chime sounded and Kaylee turned to Mary. "Do you mind seeing who that is?"

"Sure," Mary replied. Once she got behind Alicia she made a face at the woman's back.

Kaylee lowered her gaze so Alicia wouldn't see her smile. Even Mary, who had a kind word for everyone, got perturbed at Alicia's airs. As much as she'd like to pretend otherwise, Alicia was simply a small-town girl like everyone else who grew up in Turtle Cove.

Once, after an especially harrowing appointment with Alicia, Mary had told Kaylee that Alicia had never planned to stay on the island. When she was a teen, she dreamed of going to Los Angeles to become an actress or to New York to become a model. Instead, she'd stayed on the island and started up an event planning business. *And she seems rather bent out of shape about it.*

Kaylee supposed the Edgars/Stratford wedding had been as much a boon for Alicia's business as it had been for The Flower Patch and even Jessica's Death by Chocolate bakery. None of them expected to work on such a large event. This was almost a once in a lifetime opportunity for the small business owners.

But such thoughts seemed disloyal, even wrong. What did it matter if The Flower Patch now lost revenue when a man was dead and a friend was heartbroken?

"I urged Brooke to choose the same flowers as the governor's daughter, you know," Alicia said, breaking into Kaylee's thoughts. Her voice lowered to a conspiratorial whisper. "I couldn't believe it when Brooke said she wanted the more traditional choices. Even meadow flowers. So unimaginative."

"I remember." The consultation had taken hours as Alicia alternately sweet-talked and bullied Brooke into making the decisions Alicia wanted her to make. But Kaylee had in mind a little trick of her own. The bridal bouquet would be the flowers Alicia wanted since those were the ones Brooke eventually ordered. But Kaylee had planned to incorporate a few sprigs of lavender along with the lace handkerchief Brooke had insisted be a part of the bouquet. On that issue, she hadn't budged despite Alicia's displeasure.

"I hate to say it, but Brooke's taste leaves much to be desired." Alicia rolled her eyes. "If I hadn't been there to guide her, Brooke's wedding would have been the talk of the town for all the wrong reasons. Do you know her initial color scheme was—"

"Aqua, cherry red, and khaki," came an unexpected voice from the doorway.

Alicia looked toward the speaker and gasped. "What are you doing here?"

8

Brooke fixed a steely look on the wedding planner. "My palette was meant to be retro and fun. But I let you talk me into silver and black instead."

"Silver and ebony," Alicia corrected. "With amethyst accents. Nothing could be more elegant. Besides, aqua isn't a good color for you, Brooke."

Kaylee considered this logic to be, well, illogical. Aqua was a good color for everyone. Not that it would do any good to point that out to Alicia.

Instead, Kaylee offered a welcoming smile to Brooke. "Come on in," she said warmly, then looked aghast at the flowers spread across the table. She turned back to Brooke who was staring at the arrangements. "Maybe we should go somewhere else. My office, perhaps?"

"No," Brooke said firmly. "I'm fine."

"I thought you were in jail," Alicia said.

"Alicia!" Kaylee couldn't hide the shock in her voice. Did the woman have no compassion?

"I have a good attorney."

"Tyler Stevens?" Alicia sneered. "How forgiving he is."

"Alicia, I don't think—" Kaylee began.

Brooke held up her hand. "It's okay, Kaylee. Alicia's right. Tyler has been more of a friend to me than I deserve. I'll never be able to repay his kindness."

"Of course I'm glad he managed to get you out of jail," Alicia said. "But you have bigger things to worry about than talking to your vendors. I told you I'd take care of all the details."

Brooke pointedly turned her attention from Alicia to Kaylee. "I don't expect a refund."

"We're going over the bill now," Alicia said hurriedly. "Many of these flowers can be used for other orders or sold at a discount."

Brooke picked up one of the centerpieces. Variegated irises and white roses filled an amethyst vase engraved with silver filigree. "I think these would brighten up the dining room tables at the nursing home. Could you take care of that for me, Kaylee?"

A small lump caught in Kaylee's throat at Brooke's thoughtfulness in the midst of her sorrow. "I'd be happy to."

"The rest can be donated to the hospital. Or wherever else is appropriate." A faraway look appeared in Brooke's eyes. "A final gift from James."

The lump in Kaylee's throat expanded as any lingering doubts she might have had of Brooke's guilt disappeared. If only Sheriff Maddox was here. If he could see Brooke now, even he would have to admit she hadn't killed her fiancé.

But Alicia's impatience ended the poignant moment. "You can't seriously—" she sputtered.

"I think that takes care of things here," Brooke interrupted.

"I guess it does." Alicia made a point of jabbing a brown fingernail against her tablet's screen. "Another item off my list of messes to clean up with this canceled wedding. Only fifty more to go."

Neither Kaylee nor Brooke spoke while Alicia slid the tablet into her bag and stalked out.

"You would think the money came from her pocket," Brooke said after the door closed behind Alicia. "I'm sorry she's such a pain." She crouched to greet Bear, who had trotted over to sniff her. "Hey, little guy. I'm glad you're feeling better," she said, giving him a welcome scratch behind the ears.

"Alicia's behavior is not your fault," Kaylee said. "How are you, Brooke? Really?"

"Happy to be out of that jail." Her gaze focused on Kaylee. "Do you know Tyler Stevens?"

"We've met a couple of times." The last time he'd been in The Flower Patch, he had bought a dozen pink roses for Brooke. But that had been months ago, before she and James became an item.

"And Kathy Fitz?"

"The librarian?"

"They're waiting for us in your consultation room. Tyler wants to talk to you."

"To me? Why?"

"I'll let him explain."

Kaylee tried to come up with a reason for Tyler's visit. Perhaps he wanted to talk about the photograph pieces she'd found. She steeled herself for that possibility. No matter how much he tried to persuade her to give them to Brooke, she had to show them to Sheriff Maddox. That was the next to-do item on her agenda.

More surprising than Tyler's presence was that of Kathy Fitz. She was several years older than Kaylee and had worked in the local school district before taking over the Orcas Island Library. As head librarian, she had upgraded the library's computer capabilities and instituted several popular programs. But why was she here with Brooke?

Kaylee let Brooke lead the way to the cozy consultation area, following behind her with Bear cuddled against her chest. Furnished with comfortable seating and attractive occasional tables, the Victorian mansion's former parlor was now the perfect place for customers to peruse color schemes, floral designs, and embellishments.

Mary, bless her heart, had served coffee to their guests. Kathy had her long dark hair pulled back into a bun, but that was her only nod to the stereotype of the plain librarian. Tall and slim, she carried herself with poise. Her deep brown eyes exuded intelligence and confidence, and she favored bright clothing with modern patterns. Kaylee had heard it said that Kathy knew more of the town's secrets than any of the other residents and that she never broke a confidence. Other libraries had offered her larger salaries and enticing perks, but she loved Orcas Island too much to ever leave.

When Brooke and Kaylee entered, Tyler stood and offered Brooke the chair beside him. She gave him a grateful but weary smile. As soon as she was seated, exhaustion seemed to weigh upon her shoulders. She accepted Mary's offer of hazelnut coffee and wrapped her hands around the mug as if she couldn't get enough of its warmth.

Kaylee's heart went out to the younger woman. She couldn't imagine the burden she must be carrying. If she had been in Brooke's shoes, Kaylee would be kicking them off and burying herself under one of Bea's homemade quilts at Wildflower Cottage, and she wouldn't emerge from the bed for anyone or anything.

"Thanks for the coffee, Mary," Kathy said as she rose from her seat. "I thought I'd pick up a few soaps and lotions while I'm here. Maybe even treat myself to a small arrangement of daisies."

"Let me show you some items we've gotten in since the last time you were here," Mary said. "DeeDee has a new selection of handcrafted goat milk soap on display. It's especially creamy and has the most delicate fragrance."

"That woman is so talented," Kathy said as they headed out of the room. "I don't suppose she milks the goats herself?"

Mary laughed. "She gets the milk from a local farmer. But if they did have goats, I think she'd leave the milking to Andy."

"Then he could churn butter to sell at his organic market. I wonder what goat butter tastes like."

"And he could make goat cheese."

"Oh, I love goat cheese!"

The two women continued to chat, their voices diminishing to a murmur, and then they were out of earshot.

Kaylee added a packet of unrefined sugar to her coffee, then joined Brooke and Tyler at the square table in front of the large window. She loved that spot in the room, and it seemed her customers were often drawn to it too with all the natural light.

Tyler cleared his throat and said, "Thank you for agreeing to speak with us, Ms. Bleu."

Brooke placed her hand on his arm. "You don't need to use your lawyer voice," she said softly.

He slightly reddened then cleared his voice again. "We need your help," he said simply.

"What can I do?" Kaylee asked.

"I've done my homework. I know you helped the Seattle police with more than a few investigations while you were at the university."

"I did what I could."

"Don't be modest," Brooke said. "You're amazing."

"I wouldn't say that."

"You know more about plants—specifically poisonous plants—than anyone else around here," Tyler said.

"I suppose."

He leaned closer. "Sheriff Maddox said you identified the poison in James's tea as oleander. Is that true?"

"I'm not sure I'm supposed to share that information."

"Perhaps not," Brooke said. "But it's already all over town."

"For the sake of argument," Tyler said, "let's assume what everyone already knows to be true is true. I have only one question for you."

"What's that?" Kaylee asked.

"Can you tell if the poison found in James's mug came from a specific plant?"

"Theoretically, yes. But despite what everyone 'already knows,' the crime lab hasn't confirmed the poison was oleander."

"So you could theoretically test the plant they found in Brooke's garage? See if it's a match to the specific plant that contributed to the poisoned honey?"

"Perhaps. But if it's a match, wouldn't that prove Brooke's guilt?"

"It wasn't her plant." Tyler clenched then relaxed his fist. "But if we could find where it came from, the parent plant if you will, maybe we could find out who hid it in Brooke's garage."

"Who knows how many oleander plants are on this island?" Kaylee's mind raced. "That's supposing the poison was local."

"I believe it is," Tyler replied. "And I'm pretty sure I know where to find it."

Kaylee stared at him in surprise. "Have you told the sheriff?"

"I'd rather tell you."

Before Kaylee could answer, Brooke spoke up. "It's just a hunch, Kaylee, and the sheriff only deals in facts. I find it hard to believe myself, but if Tyler is right and you can identify the parent plant, maybe Sheriff Maddox will leave me alone. Please say you'll try."

"I'm not sure the sheriff wants me involved with the investigation beyond what I've already done."

"I could hire you as a consultant," Tyler said. "He couldn't stop you then."

Kaylee looked around the room as if she could find an answer to whether she should accept Tyler's offer somewhere on the walls. If Tyler was right and she could find out where the plant came from, perhaps they could discover the identity of the true murderer.

And Kaylee was ninety-nine percent sure that it wouldn't be Brooke Edgars.

She took another sip of her coffee, not because she wanted it, but because she needed time to think. Trying to find the so-called parent plant on Orcas Island would be worse than sifting through a bale of hay in search of the proverbial needle. She didn't want to disappoint Brooke or Tyler. But there was a giant elephant in the room, and someone needed to confront it.

"Even if we find where the plant came from, it doesn't prove you weren't the one who poisoned the tea. Are you sure you want me to test the oleander plant found in your house?" she asked quietly.

"I wish you could," Brooke said. Her eyes were large and worried. "But Sheriff Maddox took it to the Seattle crime lab before he came to get me."

"That makes sense. They have the proper equipment."

"I doubt they'll prioritize it, though," Tyler said. "It's a small-town murder on a small island. They have bigger fish to fry on the mainland. Who knows when they'll have any conclusive results? Meanwhile, Sheriff Maddox is focusing on Brooke instead of looking for the real killer. If I hired you as a consultant, I could get you access to that plant for testing. Every day Brooke is under suspicion is another day more and more people decide she's guilty."

His voice rose as he spoke. Kaylee half-expected him to pound the table, but instead he stood and paced the floor, clearly trying to calm himself.

Kaylee turned to Brooke. In the back of her mind, her initial theory still had roots—that it was Brooke, not James, who was the murderer's intended victim. "I don't want to upset you," she said at last. "But if I'm going to help then I need to know what happened that day. Before you came to the lighthouse."

"It seems I've told this story so many times."

"I know it's hard. But I'd like to hear it from you."

Brooke took a deep breath and seemed to shrink into the chair. "It was the day before our big wedding." Her voice took on a wistful tone, a young girl readying herself to tell a sad story. "I didn't want it to be a hectic, crazy day filled with taking care of last-minute details. Neither did James."

She paused, and Kaylee resisted the impulse to break the silence. This was Brooke's story, and she could take all the time she needed to tell it in her own way.

"That was one reason we hired Alicia." Brooke frowned. "Sometimes I wish we hadn't, but James said I needed to get used to people doing things for me. I'm not sure I ever could, and Alicia didn't make it easy."

She paused and held Kaylee's gaze. "I know what you're thinking—that James should have taken my side and let me make my own decisions about *my* wedding. Maybe so. But you know all those decisions about colors and flowers and dresses? None of it mattered. All that mattered was that we would be together for the rest of our lives." She gazed out the window, though Kaylee doubted Brooke saw anything but the memories of James she'd hidden in her heart. "We talked about eloping so many times."

"So you went to the diner," Kaylee finally prompted when Brooke's silence lasted too long.

"Yes," Brooke said, shaking her head as if to refocus her thoughts. "Our wedding was going to be perfect and the day before our wedding was supposed to be perfect too. We drove over to Doe Bay, you know over on the eastern side of the island, to see the sunrise. James brought a picnic breakfast."

"When did you go to the diner?" Kaylee asked.

"Shortly before we came to the lighthouse. Alicia wanted us to meet her there to go over a few items."

"That's when you ordered the tea?"

Brooke clasped her hands in her lap and avoided Kaylee's gaze. "Yes. I ordered the tea and James ordered a lemonade."

Tyler returned to the table. "Sheriff Maddox thinks Brooke added the poison to James's tea when he stepped out to take a call."

"Wait a minute," Kaylee said. "Wasn't James drinking the lemonade?"

"I got a refill on the tea before we left and added my honey to it. James poured it in his travel mug so we could take it with us." She smiled in memory. "He always carried that thing. He was very health conscious and tried to drink sixty-four ounces of water every day."

"Has the lab confirmed that the honey in the mug came from the jar you were carrying?" Kaylee asked.

"Not yet," Tyler said. "Like I said, a small-town murder isn't a priority for them. It may be another week or two before we get their results."

"I didn't know there was poison in the jar, Kaylee," Brooke said.

"I believe you."

If anything, that piece of evidence was too obvious, as if the murderer wanted to frame Brooke. But if that was true, then her initial theory was wrong. As far as Kaylee knew, James had been drinking the tea that was supposedly Brooke's, and Brooke hadn't touched it. A prosecutor would suggest that she wasn't drinking the tea because she knew it was poisoned. Between that and the oleander plant found at her place, it would look very much like Brooke had killed James. Why would the murderer try to kill Brooke and frame her too? That didn't make any sense at all. Besides, how would a murderer have been able to predict that James would drink the tea, not Brooke?

"Anyone who knows Brooke knows she always carries that little jar of honey with her," Tyler said. "Which is why I know where to find the oleander plant."

"Yes, you mentioned that earlier. Where do you think it came from?" Kaylee asked.

"Tim Slade's property."

"Who is Tim Slade?"

"He's a beekeeper," Brooke said. "I buy my honey from him."

Kaylee looked from Brooke to Tyler and back again. "Then why would he want to kill James and frame you?"

"Because he was furious with James," Tyler said. He leaned forward, eager to tell this part of the story. "James owns land adjacent to Slade's place. He bought it years ago, and now it seemed the time was right to develop it. But the project he was planning required about a hundred more acres. He offered Slade a good price, but it didn't matter. Slade refused to sell. Said the land had been in his family for generations and he wasn't going to be the one to part with even an acre."

"It sounds to me like James was the one with motive then, not Mr. Slade."

"There's more. Slade wouldn't listen to reason and he wasn't interested in money. So James asked me to do a title search. That's when things got iffy. The Slades have been claiming that land for over a hundred years, but it isn't necessarily theirs."

"But surely if the family had been paying taxes—"

Tyler held up both hands. "Don't you see? It didn't really matter. The title wasn't clean, and that gave James the leverage he needed. He offered Slade a choice: Either sell the land, still at a very good price, or face a lawsuit. James knew Slade couldn't afford a long, drawn-out trial. It was just a matter of time before the property became his."

Kaylee kept her expression impassive but inside her stomach churned with growing anger toward James. Apparently Brooke saw a different side to the man, but it was incidents like this that created enemies. Why couldn't James have left Mr. Slade alone?

Did the island really need a huge development project?

The answer to that question was easy—absolutely not.

If Tim Slade felt the same way, perhaps killing James was the only option he thought was available to him. But why frame Brooke?

"Is there oleander on Mr. Slade's property?" Kaylee finally asked.

"There has to be," Tyler retorted. "He put it in Brooke's honey jar."

"Are you saying he tried to kill Brooke too?" Kaylee shook her head. "How could he have known that it would be James, not Brooke, who drank the tea?"

Tyler shrugged. "Who knows what he was thinking? The guy is crazy. Living out there in the middle of nowhere with a bunch of bees. There's a reason you don't know who he is. The man's practically a hermit."

"I'm just not sure I agree with your theory," Kaylee said. "It seems to have a lot of holes."

"James had other enemies too, you know," Tyler said. "A lot of people didn't like him."

"Jealous people," Brooke said. "He grew up thinking he had to put on a front, be this ruthless businessman who only cared about adding more money to the family's bank account. But that wasn't the real James. He did so much that no one ever knew about."

Tyler placed his hand over Brooke's. "Few people knew him like you and I did," he said, his entire demeanor changing from belligerent to gentle. "We were the fortunate ones."

Tears sprang to Brooke's eyes and she gave Tyler a grateful smile. Tyler smiled back and Kaylee caught the glint in his eyes.

With a sudden surety, she knew. Tyler was still in love with Brooke. Could he have wanted James out of the way? But then, why take a chance on Brooke drinking the poisoned tea?

9

Kaylee washed the last coffee cup in the shop's kitchenette area, hoping the task would take her mind from the conversation with Tyler and Brooke, who had just left. Mary joined her. "What was that all about?" she asked.

Kaylee picked up a towel and started drying the mugs she had washed. "They want my help finding the specific oleander plant the poison came from."

"Can you do that?"

"Maybe. I don't know." Kaylee set down a dry mug and picked up a wet one. "But it's not like I can test every oleander plant on the island. And even if I did somehow miraculously find the right plant, the evidence might not hold up in court. Forensic botany is still a young field."

"I only hope the real murderer is found," Mary said.

"You think Brooke is innocent?"

"Kathy Fitz does. Brooke is staying with her now."

"Oh?" Kaylee dried another mug.

"That's the deal Tyler worked out with the court and Sheriff Maddox. Kathy is acting as a kind of guardian to make sure Brooke doesn't leave town again."

"I didn't know Brooke and Kathy were such good friends."

"I didn't either," Mary said. "But I trust Kathy's judgment, and she obviously trusts Brooke."

"I wonder if Kathy knows something we don't," Kaylee said as she placed the last mug on the tray to return to the consulting area.

"Could be. Brooke was with her Saturday night when she told Jess she planned to spend the evening home alone."

The door chimes sounded, followed by a familiar, "Hello?"

"We're back here," Kaylee called.

Jessica came into the room. "Busy?"

"Were your ears burning?" Kaylee teased. "We were just talking about you. Kind of."

"Nothing good, I hope," Jessica said lightly. "You know I seem to have a reputation for being a goody-two-shoes."

"That's because you are a goody-two-shoes." Mary laughed and picked up the tray of clean coffee mugs. "I'll take these back to the consultation room."

"Thanks," Kaylee said. "Then we can put the floral arrangements for the nursing home in my SUV. I'll drop them off if you can tend the store while I'm gone."

"I've got nowhere else to be," Mary said with a grin, then disappeared with the tray.

"The nursing home?" Jessica asked.

"Brooke wants to donate her wedding flowers. I said I'd deliver them."

"That's sweet of her. And just like Brooke. Always putting others first, even during a difficult time."

"I don't think Alicia was very happy about it."

"I confess that's why I came over."

Kaylee gave her a quizzical look. "What?"

"I saw Brooke stop in with her entourage, and I had to find out what was going on."

Kaylee grinned. Leave it to Jessica to bring a breath of fresh air and levity into a bleak situation. "I hardly call Tyler Stevens and Kathy Fitz an entourage."

"Come on, Kaylee. Tell me why they were here." Jessica put her hands on her hips and pretended to glare. "And what were you and Mary saying about me when I came in?"

"Only that when Brooke told you she was spending Saturday

night alone, she actually stayed with Kathy."

"That's odd. I didn't know they were close."

"Neither did we."

"What else did you talk about? It seemed like they were here forever. I thought they'd never leave."

"Come help me load the flowers, and I'll tell you everything I can." Talking to her best friend might just be what Kaylee needed right now to help her get to the bottom of this mystery.

Somehow she needed either to clear Brooke's name or—as much as she hated to even think it—find definitive proof of Brooke's guilt. Then she and everyone else in the community could go back to preparing for the next big influx of tourists.

If they weren't all scared away by murder.

As they ferried floral arrangements back and forth from the shop to her SUV, Kaylee relayed everything she had learned from Tyler and Brooke to Jessica, who chimed in now and again with a murmur of surprise.

"That's the whole story," Kaylee said as they put the last box of flowers into the back of the Ford Escape.

"Do you really think Tyler is in love with Brooke?"

"He seems to be. He's certainly doing everything he can to prove she's innocent."

Jessica stood quietly for a bit, obviously deep in thought. Then her face lit up. "Then that's the answer."

"What is?"

"Tyler killed James so he could have another chance with Brooke," Jessica said.

"I wondered about that too," Kaylee said. "But then why would he try to frame her with that plant in her garage? Besides, what if she drank the tea? No, he wouldn't take that chance."

"I guess you're right." Jessica's forehead furrowed in thought, then her eyes lit up. "Unless somehow he knew she wouldn't drink it. And he framed her so he could prove she was innocent. The knight in shining armor rescuing the damsel in distress."

"And then the knight goes to prison for murder?" Kaylee shook her head but couldn't help laughing. Jessica's theories were usually outlandish, but they were always good for entertainment.

Such close friendships, developed so quickly, made Kaylee thankful that she had been brave enough to uproot herself and move to Turtle Cove. She had agonized over the decision of whether she should buy her grandmother's home and business. But despite the grief she'd endured after finding out the truth concerning Grandpa's death, she was glad she'd overcome her fears and taken the chance. Just talking to Jessica about her conversation with Brooke and Tyler, and hearing what she had to say, had lightened Kaylee's spirits.

"Maybe Tyler didn't mean to frame Brooke," Jessica said.

"But the poison is in Brooke's honey jar. The same jar she takes everywhere she goes. It's like I said before. Tyler wouldn't risk poisoning Brooke. Especially if he is in love with her."

"I guess Tyler wouldn't have put the oleander plant in Brooke's house either. Unless," Jessica continued, apparently too excited about her theory to let a little detail like that stand in the way, "he wanted to throw suspicion off himself."

"And onto Brooke? I don't think so."

"Tyler is a lawyer, and he knows that all this evidence is only circumstantial. So Brooke is blamed, Tyler defends her so brilliantly the jury finds her not guilty, and—again—he's the hero. Brooke is overcome with gratitude and the next thing we know, we're all planning another wedding."

"Oh, Jess. Do you really believe that?"

"Stranger things have happened. Don't you ever read the online news?"

Kaylee gave her friend a look. "Most of which is made up."

Jessica refused to be dissuaded. "People are complicated beings. For all we know, Tyler never meant for things to get as far as they did. But from where I'm standing, he's got a good thing going. Brooke is emotionally distraught, vulnerable. And he's her hero."

"Sounds like you've got it all figured out." Kaylee headed back into the flower shop for Bear and her bag. Jessica followed her. "It's getting late and I need to talk to Sheriff Maddox after I deliver these flowers."

"Why are you seeing the sheriff?"

"To show him a photograph I found on the beach." She dug through her bag and drew out the two specimen bags. "Do you recognize these girls?"

Jessica looked at the photo and smiled. "Brooke and her cousin, Beth. They were friends with Mila as children. Remember? I told you that the other day."

"I remember."

"Especially Beth." Jessica seemed lost in memory for a few seconds. "Brooke was often ill. She seemed to get every cold, every virus that came around. As if her immune system wasn't very strong."

"You'd never know that to look at her now."

"I guess she grew out of it. Anyway, Beth frequently stayed with us when Brooke was ill, and she and Mila were very close." Jessica looked at the photo halves again. "You said you found these on the beach? How did they get there?"

"That's the mystery, isn't it? I showed them to Brooke yesterday, but she doesn't remember ever seeing the photo before. At least that's what she said."

"That's odd." Jessica turned the bags over. "Kodak paper. But that doesn't tell us anything, does it? Lots of photos are developed with Kodak. At least they used to be."

Mary joined them. "Two more arrangements for the funeral," she said as she placed the order forms on the work flow board. "We're going to be busy."

"I appreciate the extra hours you're putting in," Kaylee said. "You're such a big help."

"I don't mind," Mary said. "Keeps me occupied."

"Just know how much I appreciate it." Kaylee returned the photograph halves to her bag. "If I don't get going, I'll never get back. Come on, Bear. Let's go for a ride."

The little dachshund jumped around Kaylee's legs, then raced toward the back door.

Jessica smiled at Bear's antics. "You'd never know he spent a night in the equivalent of a doggy ICU a few days ago, would you?"

"He's a little trooper." Kaylee jangled her keys with one hand and scooped up Bear with the other. "See you later, ladies."

All during her short drive from the flower shop to the nursing home, Kaylee replayed her conversation with Brooke and Tyler. She also pondered what Jessica had to say. Maybe Tyler did have a hero complex.

Or maybe there was another explanation. What if his concern for Brooke was all a ruse? By killing James and framing Brooke, he could get vengeance on both of them for hurting him. His story about a feud between James and Tim Slade could be a smoke screen, something to keep everyone's attention focused on anyone else but Tyler.

It was plausible, but Kaylee had no idea how to find out if Tyler was the murderer. If he had poisoned James, he was doing a great job of covering his tracks.

Brooke had scooped poisoned honey from her jar into the tea. Sheriff Maddox had mentioned that the waitress at the diner had told him she watched her do it, had seen her do it multiple times. But that didn't mean Brooke knew the honey was poisonous. Tyler could have switched the jars. Which meant he would have had to buy a jar just like Brooke's.

From Tim Slade, the beekeeper.

Could this be another clue?

Kaylee delivered the flowers then set out for the sheriff's headquarters in Eastsound. On the way out of Turtle Cove, she passed the street where Rick Saunders's photography studio was located.

Suddenly it occurred to her that Rick could tell her something about the photograph. He was about Brooke's age and had grown up on the island. She needed to show it to him now in case the sheriff kept it as evidence, which he probably would. She went around the block and parked in front of his studio. Then she strode purposefully into the gallery with Bear in her arms.

"So this is the famous Bear," Rick said in greeting. "Sorry I haven't called to schedule his photo shoot. How's next week?"

"Should be fine, but that's not why I'm here," Kaylee said. "I have something to show you."

"If this has anything to do with my portrait of Brooke—"

"No. Why would it?"

"Never mind." He gave her a broad smile and rested his palms on the counter. "What can I do for you?"

Kaylee placed the two bags on the counter. Rick glanced at the photo halves and his face paled. He cleared his throat and coughed as he tried to regain his composure. "Where did you get these?"

"I found them on the beach."

"They have nothing to do with me."

"Who said they did?"

"Why else would you bring them here?"

"To see if you know the girls."

"Sure," he said, his voice congenial again. "Brooke and Beth. We all went to school together. Different grades, since James and I are a couple of years older, but Brooke and I were in the same art class for a couple of years. James and Alicia too."

"I didn't know Brooke and James were artists. Alicia either for that matter." Perhaps she had channeled her creativity into event planning. Come to think of it, she had treated the Edgars/ Stratford wedding as a giant tableau. Her eye for color when it came to choosing ribbons and embellishments for the flower arrangements and even the cake had been spot-on. Only her manners in deferring to the bride's preferences needed improving.

"James was a dabbler," Rick said dismissively. "Brooke had real talent, though. The three of us—Brooke, Alicia, and me—seemed to take turns winning the top prizes in the local art competitions."

"Sometimes it's hard to be friends with people you're competing against."

"Sometimes."

Kaylee waited for Rick to say more, but he pressed his lips together and stared at her. She suspected he knew more than he was saying, but he obviously wasn't going to tell her anything else. At least not voluntarily.

"Were you? Friends, I mean?"

"We were kids."

"A grudge can last a long time."

"Are you trying to accuse me of something?"

Taken aback by his direct question, Kaylee straightened as if bracing herself. Not that she believed he would take any physical action, but she wanted to mentally prepare herself for any verbal assault he might throw at her. After all, she didn't know him well enough to be able to predict what he would or wouldn't do.

"No," she said at last. "More thinking out loud."

"You think James was murdered because of something that happened when we were kids? Because we were in the same art class?"

"It sounds ludicrous when you put it like that."

"You think?" He snorted. "Look, Kaylee. I understand that you think you're a part of this community because your grandparents spent most of their lives here. But just because you live in your grandmother's house and own your grandmother's business doesn't mean you have carte blanche to stick your nose into other people's business around here."

"All I'm trying to do is figure out who killed James. Because I don't believe it was Brooke."

His gaze turned inscrutable, and Kaylee sensed he was taking her measure. Finally he slid the photo halves across the counter to her. "She didn't."

"You know that for sure?"

"I know it for sure."

"How?"

His mouth formed a tight line and the expression in his eyes flattened.

"What did you mean earlier?" Kaylee asked, changing tactics. "Why did you think I was here about Brooke's portrait?"

He hesitated. Then his eyes brightened and one corner of his mouth turned up slightly. "It's a good likeness, isn't it?"

"It's breathtaking."

He seemed pleased by the compliment. "One of the best portraits I've ever done."

"Then why—"

"Something someone else said. I'm not sure what's going to happen to it, that's all."

"Brooke doesn't want it?"

"Would you?"

Kaylee tried to imagine losing the love of her life the day before her wedding, then being offered the painting of herself that had been made to hang next to the portrait of him in their home together. "Probably not."

"I'll see you next week, Kaylee." His dismissive tone let her know she'd overstayed her welcome. Rick shifted his gaze from her to Bear. His face softened and his tone lightened. "And your little dog too," he added in a passable impression of the Wicked Witch of the West. "How about next Monday morning?"

"You can't tell me anything else about this photo?" Kaylee said quickly.

"It's old." He walked toward the hallway leading from the gallery. Before going through the door, he paused. "Taken about fifteen years ago, I'd say."

"Brooke told me she didn't remember seeing it before."

He slightly turned toward Kaylee, his expression unreadable. "Maybe it wasn't hers."

"You mean it belonged to Beth? Then how did it end up on the beach?"

"Does it matter?" He heaved a deep sigh. "You're not one of us, Kaylee, and you never will be. So stop trying."

Before she could respond, he disappeared and closed the hall door firmly behind him. Kaylee stood alone in the gallery as she tried to process everything that had been said. But she could hardly concentrate on anything she'd learned about Brooke. She was distracted by Rick's dislike for her.

Where did that come from?

Just because she didn't grow up in Turtle Cove was no reason for him to be so dismissive. She'd spent lots of time here with her grandparents as a child. She knew the town, the island, many of the longtime residents. This place had always been her second home. And now it was her first home. Her only home.

She tried not to let Rick's words hurt her, but they did. They made her feel small, unwanted. Kind of how she'd felt when she was forced out of the university after devoting so many years of her life to teaching. She'd loved her profession until all the politics had become too much for her. At the end, she'd been glad to leave, although a piece of her heart would always be in academia and she would always treasure memories of her favorite students. Making a new start had been a hard thing to do, even if it seemed like it had been the smart, the wise, the prudent, and the best thing to do.

She loved it here in Turtle Cove. She might not be a native, but her roots here ran very deep. Arguably much deeper than Rick Saunders's given her Quinault heritage. Holding her head high, she walked out of the studio and headed for her car. It was past time to talk to Sheriff Maddox.

10

In no time at all Kaylee arrived at the sheriff's office in Eastsound. Her thoughts had been so preoccupied with all the conversations she'd had that day—with Brooke and Tyler, with Mary and Jessica, with Rick—that it seemed she had driven there on autopilot, in spite of the scenic route provided along the main road on the island. This wasn't a day for sightseeing. After meeting with Rick, she was despondent and tired. Now that she was at the station, all she wanted was to show Sheriff Maddox the two halves of the torn photograph and go home.

She had a small casserole dish of homemade macaroni and cheese in the refrigerator—the perfect comfort food after such a long day. Maybe she'd eat outside and get a fire going in the fire pit, or settle in a comfy chair in the sunroom with that new mystery DeeDee had recommended. She'd said it was fantastic with a very unexpected plot twist.

Then again, if the plot included murder, Kaylee wasn't in the mood. Why couldn't DeeDee specialize in romances instead of murder mysteries? Not that Kaylee was in the mood for a romance either. It would just make her think of Brooke's heartache all over again.

No bride should lose the man she loved the day before her wedding. Whoever killed James should be given an additional punishment for such hateful timing. Perhaps the traditional wedding march could be continually piped into the murderer's prison cell—a constant reminder of the happiness whoever it was had spoiled.

"That would serve him right, wouldn't it, Bear?" Kaylee grimaced. "Or her."

Bear yipped in reply.

"I'm glad you agree with me." She unbuckled the straps from his pet safety seat and lifted him out. "Maybe we'll find a movie to watch instead. Something light and funny. But not *Lady and the Tramp*. You know how scared you are of that nasty rat."

She started to open her car door then stopped. "Sorry, Bear. One more thing I need to do before we go in. If Sheriff Maddox decides he wants to keep these," she waved the photograph halves, "I want to have a copy." She arranged the two pieces on the console between the seats and snapped a couple of photos with her phone's camera. "Now we can go."

Once inside headquarters, Kaylee approached the receptionist's desk. Though she did her best not to sniff, she couldn't help it. Aida Friedman's pack-a-day habit created a distinctive, perpetual smell around her work area. Who would have ever thought wintergreen Tic Tacs could be so overpowering? Or that anyone would choose Tic Tacs for a vice.

Kaylee preferred Aida's other obsession—her regular stops at The Flower Patch to pick up an assortment of dyed carnations. She always brought Bear a treat too. Kaylee might have to put a *Don't Feed the Bear* sign on her store counter to keep the little guy from becoming a sausage roll.

Aida glanced at Kaylee, held up a finger to indicate that she'd be with her shortly, and hit a few more keys on her keyboard. The printer nearby whirred to life and spit out paper.

She turned her attention back to Kaylee and her companion. "Hi, Bear," she said enthusiastically. "Back in action, it looks like."

"He's much better, thanks," Kaylee said.

"I about fainted when I heard what happened to him." As if to emphasize her words, Aida fanned herself with her fingers. "You must have been frantic with worry. If something like that happened to one of my fur babies"—Aida took in a deep breath, and her light blue eyes widened behind her designer frames—"I think they'd have to put me in a kennel right next to them. I'm just not sure I'd ever survive."

"I admit I was scared," Kaylee said, Aida's dramatics bringing a smile to her lips. Everyone knew the receptionist adored her three cats—a diluted calico who'd been found in a fast-food parking lot when she was only days old, a feisty snow-white Persian who spent her first two years in a cage before Aida rescued her, and a gray tabby who'd wandered into the police station one day apparently on a whim—but it was hard to take her "about to collapse any moment" attitude seriously. After all, come Thursday night, Aida would be skating around the roller derby rink in Seattle where she was known to her longtime fans as Miss Demeanor.

"Thankfully, Dr. Melody is a talented veterinarian."

"And . . .?" Aida said suggestively.

Kaylee narrowed her eyes in puzzlement. "And what?"

"And you had a handsome deputy who raced through town to save Bear's life."

"Well, yes," Kaylee said.

"Don't you think you ought to show him your appreciation?"

Kaylee tilted her head. "What are you getting at?"

"Oh, come on, Kaylee. Nick's a real catch. Maybe you ought to cast a line. If I didn't already have a boyfriend, I'd go after him."

"He must be at least ten years older than you."

"Thirteen." Aida reached for her Tic Tacs. "But who cares about age anymore?"

Kaylee shifted uneasily at the topic of conversation. If she was going to date anyone on the island, it certainly wouldn't be serial flirt Nick Durham. "I called Sheriff Maddox a while ago," she said, changing the subject. "I think he's expecting me."

"He told me to send you right in as soon as you got here."

And instead you kept me here talking about Nick? Thanks a lot, Miss Demeanor.

"It's been great catching up with you, Aida. Thanks."

"Don't forget what I said about Nick. A little gratitude goes a long way."

Trying to decide whether she was amused or annoyed by Aida's futile attempt to play Cupid, Kaylee headed for the sheriff's private office, content to leave the roller-derby receptionist to her computer and her Tic Tacs.

Sheriff Maddox saw Kaylee through the glass partition in his office and raised a welcoming hand. She said hello to Deputy Garcia, the only deputy around at the time. At least Nick wasn't there. He was probably out on patrol with the other officers. That was fine with her. After that conversation with Aida, she didn't want to run into him.

Inside the sheriff's office, she declined his offer of coffee and placed Bear in the seat beside her. He immediately crossed his front paws and rested his long nose on them as if to say the humans could have a conversation without any interruptions from him.

"What's so important that you came all the way up here?" Sheriff Maddox asked.

"It's not really that far," Kaylee protested mildly.

"If you'd waited till tomorrow, I could have met you in Turtle Cove."

"I know. And it probably isn't anything, but it's been weighing on my mind. I'd feel better if I told you about it. Then you could decide if it's important."

The sheriff's swivel chair creaked as he leaned back. "I'm all ears."

"I climbed up to the widow's walk yesterday after church," Kaylee began, then told him how she'd remembered seeing someone running away from the lighthouse shortly before discovering James's body. "I suppose my concern about Bear drove it from my mind. But now I wonder if that person was the murderer."

"You don't want to believe it was Brooke."

"I still think she might have been the intended victim."

"I'm not sure you aren't right about that," Sheriff Maddox said, his attention focused on her. "But this beach runner as the murderer? You're smarter than that, Kaylee."

"What do you mean?"

"I take it you think this mysterious runner was on the widow's walk with Mr. Stratford before you went up there."

If she'd been in a cartoon, this was the moment the bulb would have lit up over her head. How could she not have seen her wayward logic before?

"I can't have it both ways, can I?" she said sheepishly. Obviously if the runner was on the widow's walk, then Brooke wasn't the intended victim. But if the runner had meant to kill James, how did the poisoned honey get in the travel mug? The murderer couldn't very well have done it with James standing right beside him. Not to mention the runner would have had to get up to the widow's walk and back down without any of the Petal Pushers seeing him or her.

"You don't think the runner is important, do you?" Kaylee asked.

"He or she might be a witness. To what exactly, I couldn't say."

"Then I guess my evidence isn't important either."

"What evidence?"

"I walked along the beach, trying to follow the same path I saw the runner take." She pulled the photograph halves from her bag. "I found these under a bush. They're old, two jagged pieces of a photograph, but I don't think they'd been out in the weather for more than a couple of days. Certainly not before last Thursday's rainstorm."

"Let me see." The sheriff's chair squeaked again as he bent forward to take the evidence bags from Kaylee and studied them. "Any idea who these girls are?"

"Brooke and her cousin, Beth."

"You sure?"

"I showed them to Brooke. And to Jessica Roberts. She knew the girls when they were young. They were friends with her daughter."

"Now that you say so, I can see the resemblance to our grown-up Brooke. When was the photo taken?"

"They look to be about eleven or twelve there, so around fifteen years ago. But Brooke told me she'd never seen it before."

"That sounds odd."

"Maybe it belonged to her cousin. Or to whoever took the picture."

"Maybe the mystery photographer is our mystery runner."

Kaylee gave that some thought. She supposed Rick could have been the person she saw running that day. He'd seemed defensive when she showed him the photograph, as if he was hiding something. But why lie about an old torn-up snapshot?

"I showed it to Rick Saunders too."

"Has everyone in town seen this photograph except me?"

Kaylee slightly reddened. "I thought he might know something about it."

"Did he?"

"He said he didn't. He also said Brooke didn't kill James."

"How does he know that?"

"I couldn't tell you. He's not very friendly, but he sounded confident."

Sheriff Maddox spread his hands across his desk. "Well, I don't know if Brooke's the murderer or if she's being framed. I don't know why you are questioning people who might know something instead of leaving it to me." Kaylee ducked her head, and he continued, "I don't know if the murderer meant to kill James or to kill Brooke. I don't know much of anything about this case except that one of our most prominent citizens is dead under mysterious circumstances and somebody knows more than they're telling."

"What are you going to do?"

"Go through the evidence again. And this time, my favorite forensic botanist consultant is going to go through it with me. I might as well keep you involved since you insist on it anyway. Are you game?"

"I'm game."

"Come on then."

He led the way to a locked room, tapped numbers into the keypad, then flipped on the light as they went inside. Several filing cabinets and assorted shelves lined the walls, and a long table with metal legs was centered beneath a row of fluorescent lights. A few objects, each one in an evidence bag, were at one end of the table. A striped ceramic pot held a *Nerium oleander* plant, its thick, dark-green leaves splaying outward.

"This is all you have?" Kaylee asked, her heart sinking.

"This is it." Sheriff Maddox pointed to each item in turn. "The mug. The honey jar. The plant."

"Brooke said you took the plant to the Seattle crime lab."

"They took what they needed and sent the rest back with me." He picked up the last bag on the table and hefted it in his hand. "Here's Stratford's watch, though I'm not sure it's really evidence."

"Did you find any teeth marks on it?"

"You mean from Bear." He handed her the bag. "See for yourself, but I don't think your little wiener dog did any damage."

Kaylee examined the watch as best she could without removing it from the bag. "My fingerprints are probably all over this," she said. "It's the only reason I went up to the widow's walk that day."

"Do you wish you hadn't?"

"Sometimes. Most of the time." She gazed down at Bear, who had followed them from the office and was now sniffing around the table. "If I hadn't, Bear wouldn't have gotten sick."

"And we still might not know James's tea was poisoned." Sheriff Maddox sat on the edge of the table and fingered a long leaf from the oleander plant. "Even though this case has a high priority, it takes time for the Seattle lab to do their work. Though I'm sorry about Bear. I'm glad he's okay."

Kaylee turned her attention back to the watch.

"We've already processed it. There were no usable prints, so you can take it out if you want."

Kaylee slipped it from the bag and read the engraving. "'To T. S. Dare and Endure.' What does that mean?"

"It's another little mystery," Sheriff Maddox said. "Who is T. S.? And why did James have his watch?"

Just what this case needs, Kaylee mused. *More questions.* Wasn't it about time they discovered a few answers? Not just for James's sake, but also for Brooke's.

11

*D*are *and Endure.*

Kaylee couldn't help wondering who had chosen those words to engrave on the watch—what they were supposed to mean to the giver and to the recipient. But the greater question was the one Sheriff Maddox had asked. Why was James wearing the watch?

"Is James's first name something besides James?" she asked.

"Nope. His full name was James Garfield Stratford."

"Garfield?"

"Mother's maiden name."

"Perhaps it belonged to his father."

"You mean Matthew Allen Stratford?"

Kaylee chuckled. "Did you investigate his entire family tree?"

"The watch isn't that old. Probably dates back to about the 1980s."

"You're thorough."

Sheriff Maddox shrugged carelessly. "I had a little time on my hands." His expression clearly said, *Get it? Time on my hands.*

"Ha ha," Kaylee said. It sounded like the kind of silly joke she'd have shared with Grandpa.

A cell phone buzzed and the sheriff checked his screen. "Would you excuse me please?"

"Sure," Kaylee said.

After he left the room, she studied the watch again then glanced at the door. Flushing with nervous tension, she quickly snapped a photo of the watch's engraving. Someone had to know something about it. James was known for shopping local except when it came to luxury items he couldn't find on the island.

Maybe the watch hadn't been purchased here, but if it had ever needed service, he probably would have used a local jeweler.

Kaylee hurriedly did a search on her phone. Two jewelers were listed for Eastsound and one for Turtle Cove. Perhaps one of them would know something about the watch's history. It couldn't hurt to ask.

Three short phone calls later, she had no new information. Apparently James had not purchased the watch on the island, nor taken it to any of the jewelers for maintenance. She laid the watch on the table and systematically reviewed the rest of the evidence spread out on the table. After picking up the silver travel mug and peering at every inch of it, she gazed at the honey jar. Traces of an oleander plant had been found in the dregs of the mug and in the jar. The jar had been in Brooke's purse at the diner and had still been in her purse when she was questioned. The oleander plant at the end of the table had been found in her garage.

It was all circumstantial, and yet when taken as a whole, the evidence definitely pointed to Brooke's guilt.

Surely Brooke would have been smart enough to destroy the plant and dispose of the jar. If the silver mug was the only evidence that remained, then Brooke wouldn't be under so much suspicion.

Kaylee sighed. Even with only the mug, Brooke might be the primary suspect, but she certainly wouldn't be in as much trouble as she was now.

And yet, if she was the murderer, why had she kept the plant and the jar?

Because if Brooke was diabolical enough to create such a convoluted series of misdirections, she wasn't just smart, she was clever. The evidence was too circumstantial, too convenient. It was the very argument that Tyler had probably used to get her released on bail.

Brooke was acting like a frightened victim, but what if that's all it was—an act? Kaylee found it hard to believe, especially after meeting with her earlier.

"She didn't." Rick Saunders voice echoed in Kaylee's head. He was so sure of Brooke's innocence. But why?

Sheriff Maddox reentered the room.

"Any chance you solved the case while I was gone?" he asked.

"I wish." Kaylee placed the mug back on the table. "But I'm more confused now than I was before I got here."

He nodded slowly. "I know what you mean."

"Brooke can't be the murderer."

"I'm not sure of anything right now. And I don't like to rush to judgment on flimsy evidence. Fortunately, determining guilt or innocence is up to a jury. Not me."

"But you wouldn't arrest her unless you were confident she did it. Right?"

"My gut tells me this isn't all there is." He waved his hand toward the table, his gesture taking in all the items. "Someone is hiding something. But I'm running out of leads."

"I wish I could be of more help."

"You've done what I needed you to do. And I appreciate it." He squeezed her arm in a fatherly gesture. "But if you remember anything else or find anything that might be relevant, I want you to do me a favor."

"Tell you first?"

"That's right."

"What about the mystery runner? Shouldn't we at least try to identify him?"

"We'll do our best," he assured her. "Robyn is going to take your statement. And I'll add the photograph to the evidence list."

"But you don't think it's related to the case?"

"It's . . . odd. I grant you that. But I doubt that torn photograph is going to help me find Mr. Stratford's murderer." He stole a quick glance at the wall clock, prompting Kaylee to check the time too.

It was almost five.

"Come on, Bear," she said. "We should be getting home."

"See Robyn on your way out. It shouldn't take too long."

Kaylee nodded agreement then said goodbye. With Bear heeling beside her, she left the room and met with Deputy Garcia. True to Sheriff Maddox's word and thanks to the deputy's professional efficiency, the statement was soon ready for Kaylee's signature.

Reading her account, seeing it in black-and-white, Kaylee had to admit that the runner and the photograph halves didn't seem to amount to much. Deputy Garcia had gotten the entire event on a single page.

But it had to be more than a coincidence that a photo of Brooke was left on the beach the same day her fiancé was murdered.

Because no matter what anyone said or thought, Kaylee had a hunch that the mystery runner was the one who'd torn up the photograph and threw away the pieces. If she could only figure out "the who," then maybe she could discover "the why."

Kaylee and Bear arrived at The Flower Patch early Tuesday morning. James's funeral was the next afternoon, and Kaylee wanted plenty of time to work on all the orders that had come in. Giles Akin, the local coroner and owner of Akin Funeral Chapel, had spread the news that mourners could make a charitable donation to a local children's program or the Orcas Island Historical Society in lieu of flowers. Still, the requests kept coming in, and Kaylee fielded phone orders all morning.

After hanging up from the latest caller, she turned to Mary, who was working on the opposite side of the long work table. "That was Olivia Thomas from The Chic Boutique," Kaylee said. "She especially requested a Mary Bishop design."

"We go way back, Olivia and me. When I still worked as a police dispatcher, her mom and I were on the same shift. Olivia thinks of me as her second mother. Plus she's in my tai chi class."

Kaylee held back a sigh. Mary had celebrated her sixtieth birthday a few months ago, but she had more energy than many women half her age. Kaylee wasn't sure she could keep up with her sometimes. And her deep connections in town were suddenly enviable in light of Rick's cruel words about Kaylee being a newcomer.

"I don't know how you do everything you do," she said.

Mary smiled. "Good genetics and garden grace. You should meet my mother. Eighty-five years old with a more active social life than mine."

"Do you wish she still lived here?"

"I do. But the southern California climate is better for her health."

"What did you mean by 'garden grace'?"

"That's one of Mother's favorite expressions. Whenever anyone commented on her unusual good health, she attributed it to 'good genes and garden grace.'" Mary wrapped a ribbon around the stems of several calla lilies. "She believed that all that time she spent outdoors tending to her flowers and vegetable patch did more good than anything else in keeping her physically fit and strong."

"I like that," Kaylee said. "Garden grace." She rolled the words around in her mind. Perhaps they could use the phrase as a theme for a display in the store, one that honored the older women who first founded the Petal Pushers such as Mary's mother and Kaylee's grandmother. The ringing phone broke into Kaylee's thoughts.

She answered the call and took another order for a funeral arrangement. After hanging up, she added the latest to the others waiting to be filled.

"I don't get it," she said to Mary. "James wasn't exactly Mr. Popularity, but it seems everyone on the island wants flowers for his funeral."

"He may have had more than his share of enemies," Mary said. "But here's what you need to understand, Kaylee. James was also the last member of one of our settling families. The people here respect his heritage. This is a small way—the final way—they can honor his parents, grandparents, and all the other generations of his ancestors, back to the first Stratfords on the island."

"I didn't realize that." Kaylee stretched her back, which was starting to twinge from the hours working on her feet. "Did Brooke pick the charities for James?"

"They were in his will."

"Seems kind of odd, doesn't it? I mean James was a young man. To already have that planned out . . ."

"He probably didn't have much choice," Mary said. "I ran into Thelma Akin, Giles's wife, at the grocery store the other night. Apparently Tyler Stevens gave Giles a folder with all the necessary info about James's funeral. Sounded like it was well thought out and organized. She said Giles wishes everyone was that thorough. It would make his job much easier."

"I don't have anything like that. Do you?"

"Not really."

Kaylee's mind leaped again.

"Tyler Stevens," she murmured. "His initials are T.S."

Mary gave her a quizzical look. "They are. Is that interesting?"

"Those were the initials on the watch."

"What watch?"

"James's watch. I mean the watch James was wearing the day he was killed."

"He was wearing Tyler's watch?"

"Maybe. I don't know." Kaylee sighed deeply. "Think this through with me, Mary. Tyler is James's trusted lawyer and closest friend. He knows more about James's business dealings and his personal life than anyone else. He's dating Brooke, and he arranges for Brooke to work for James. Next thing he knows, Brooke is dumping him to be with James, and then they're planning to get married. I think he's still in love with Brooke, so I find it hard to believe he'd be okay with all of that."

"Surely you don't suspect him of being the murderer?"

"Sometimes I do and sometimes I don't."

"Even if James had Tyler's watch, that doesn't mean Tyler killed him."

"I know. But it's eating at me. Why did James have a watch with someone else's initials?"

"Why don't you ask Tyler?" Mary suggested. "After all, you just said he's the one who knew James the best. Or perhaps Brooke would know."

"Sheriff Maddox told me not to do any more investigating."

"This isn't really investigating," Mary said. "It's more like satisfying idle curiosity."

"Didn't curiosity kill the cat?"

Mary gave an elaborate shrug and scrunched up her face in a delightful teasing expression. "Maybe that's why the good Lord gave them nine lives."

By midafternoon, Kaylee had to call in reinforcements. Both Jessica and DeeDee left their employees in charge of their businesses to help Kaylee and Mary finish the floral arrangements. A florist from Sea Acre, on the eastern side of the island, was also called upon to help with the extra orders, and a vendor from the Seattle flower market arrived on the afternoon ferry with a fresh supply of blossoms, plants, greenery, and ferns. The women worked late. Around seven, DeeDee's husband, Andy, brought sandwiches from the organic grocery store he managed. They ate quickly and got back to work, fortified by the food.

Kaylee couldn't help feeling overwhelmed by the generosity of these dear women who had welcomed her so warmly into their lives and hearts. This was so unlike the cutthroat, dog-eat-dog world of academia. Once again, Kaylee could only feel gratitude for the events, hard as they had been at the time, which had forced her from the university and into the arms of the Turtle Cove community.

Rick was wrong when he said she would never be part of this place. She already was, and these women who had stepped away from their own stores—though Jessica had had to run next door a couple of times when needed at the bakery—were proof that Kaylee did belong.

Though James's murder and the question of Brooke's guilt was on everyone's mind—how could it be otherwise when they were so focused on the floral arrangements for James's funeral—they seemed to choose by silent agreement to talk of other things.

DeeDee's two daughters, eight-year-old Polly and eleven-year-old Zoe, were both practicing for a spot in the upcoming talent show sponsored by Nora Keller, the owner of Art Attack, located catty-corner from The Flower Patch. Nora and her husband, Christian, had carried on the tradition of a show spotlighting youthful artists and musicians that Nora's mother had begun ages ago. They were both passionate about the arts, as Nora was a talented painter and Christian an accomplished saxophonist who played in a jazz band.

"They wanted to do a piano duet," DeeDee was explaining as Kaylee returned to the work area after taking another order for the Stratford funeral. "But they're in different age groups."

"Didn't you win a prize once?" Mary asked DeeDee.

"When I was fifteen."

"What was your talent?" Kaylee asked.

"I'd been taking dance classes so I did my own version of 'Singing in the Rain.' Alas, my dancing career didn't make it much beyond that competition."

"Why?" Kaylee asked.

"I found something I liked better."

"What was that?"

"Andy."

The women all laughed.

"So you were high school sweethearts," Kaylee said. "I didn't know."

"Everyone said it wouldn't last, but here we are, all these years later. I think we proved the naysayers wrong." DeeDee's eyes sparkled, and she smiled as if she was still the lovestruck high school girl from years ago.

"You sure did," Jessica said. "Weren't you also named 'cutest couple' your senior year?"

"We were." DeeDee laughed. "Wow, that seems so long ago."

Kaylee focused on her work while the conversation swirled around her. She thought back to her high school days. All the dreams she'd had about marriage and children. But first and foremost, she'd wanted to learn everything she could about botany. Though she'd dated a few different boys, she couldn't imagine knowing at such a young age that any of them would have been in her life for the rest of her life. DeeDee and Andy were lucky, but that kind of relationship was also rare.

Brooke and James, so very much in love, should have had the chance to grow old together. To support each other through all the joys and sorrows of life. That had been taken away from them.

It was all so unfair.

And despite all the time Kaylee had spent mulling it over in her mind, she was no closer to solving the mystery of who had killed James Stratford. Would Brooke ever get closure?

Kaylee placed the final arrangement on the steps leading to the sanctuary's stage then went to the bathroom to wash her hands. When she returned to the foyer, Reese Holt greeted her.

"How are you doing, Kaylee?" he asked.

Though he looked more handsome than ever in a cobalt blue dress shirt that enhanced his eyes, he also seemed less like the laid-back Reese she'd come to know. The last time Kaylee had seen him this dressed up was when he'd been recruited as the best man for a hastily thrown together wedding shortly after she'd moved to Turtle Cove.

He seemed uncomfortable, as if he'd rather be anywhere else than there. She couldn't fault him for that—she felt the same way.

"A little tired from working late last night," she said. "But otherwise I'm fine. You?"

"I'm okay." He cleared his throat, seemingly searching for a safe topic of conversation. "You're looking . . . spiffy."

Spiffy?

"Um, thank you." *I think.* She glanced down at her outfit, a knee-length black skirt with a gray and black print top. Nothing flashy, but still a departure from her more casual everyday wardrobe. Perhaps she appeared as different to him as he did to her.

Reese laughed nervously. "You look nice, I mean. Sorry, I have a hard time saying the right thing at funerals. Do you want to sit together?"

"I'd like that," she said honestly, intentionally not thinking about why she found his presence comforting. He found them seats near the other Petal Pushers. Jessica caught her eye and gave a small smile, then looked pointedly at Reese. Kaylee rolled her eyes and mouthed, "Behave."

The organist started playing a selection of hymns and the crowd settled. Brooke walked up the center aisle accompanied by Kathy Fitz and Tyler Stevens. Seeing the lawyer was the only excuse Kaylee needed to let her thoughts roam wild. After Jessica's silent teasing, she was too aware of Reese's presence beside her.

Tyler Stevens. T.S.

But what, if anything, does the watch have to do with James's murder?

She shook away the unanswerable questions and focused on Brooke. The poor girl had never gotten the chance to wear her designer bridal gown. Instead, only four days after what was supposed to be the happiest day of her life, she wore a chic black dress with matching jacket. A small hat with veiled netting perched on her head. Her face was pale, but she kept her shoulders back, her posture straight.

Three other couples followed Brooke and Tyler to the reserved seats at the front of the sanctuary.

"Who are they?" Kaylee whispered to Reese.

"James's executive team," Reese whispered back.

"It's so sad that he doesn't have any family here. Isn't there even a distant cousin?"

"Not that I ever heard of. Brooke was his family."

Strange that Brooke didn't have any family here to mourn

with her either. Kaylee felt a sudden disliking for Brooke's cousin, Beth. What was so important that she couldn't have been here in Brooke's time of need?

How lonely Brooke must feel, and how alone.

Except for Tyler Stevens.

T. S.

12

After the funeral, Kaylee and Reese offered their condolences to Brooke. Her expression remained stoic as if she'd spent all her emotions and didn't have any tears left to shed.

"I need your advice, Kaylee," she said with a wave toward the sanctuary. "All those flowers. People weren't supposed to send flowers."

"I think they wanted to show their respect," Kaylee said.

"What am I supposed to do with all of them?"

Kaylee exchanged a glance with Reese, but he merely shrugged. "Do you want them taken to your house?" she asked.

Brooke's eyes widened in horror.

"Or they could go to the Stratford estate," Reese offered quickly. "I'd be glad to do that for you."

"Is that what you want, Brooke?" Kaylee asked.

Brooke's stoicism wavered, but then determination hardened her features.

"Take them to the lighthouse." Her voice lacked any warmth. "That's where I saw him last, that's where he died, and that's where we were supposed to get married. Display them in public. Perhaps then his killer will feel guilty enough to confess."

Kaylee avoided looking at Reese again. She was startled by the coldness in Brooke's voice and behind her idea. *But doesn't James's killer deserve it?*

"As soon as everyone leaves the church," Reese said softly, "I'll take the flowers to the lighthouse for you, Brooke."

She nodded her thanks.

"Are you sure you don't want to keep any of them?" Kaylee asked.

"Only the cards. I'll need to write thank-you notes." Brooke's voice cracked with grief. "I'm not sure I can bear to ever have flowers again."

Kaylee quickly scanned the various arrangements. Some were quite large, beautiful but showy. Not at all what Brooke would want. Then she spotted a tasteful arrangement of *Lavandula angustifolia* and ferns in a crystal vase. She handed it to Brooke. "Take these," she suggested. "You and James had your engagement photos taken in the lavender fields. Keep this as a happy memory, not a sad one."

Brooke eyed Kaylee as she accepted the vase. "You're right," she said. "I've always loved lavender. I still do. And I'll always remember your kindness, your thoughtfulness, whenever I see them."

Kaylee hugged her around the flowers. "There's tons of lavender outside my house. Let me know when you need a refill or if you ever want to just sit and look at it, okay?"

"Thank you so much, Kaylee."

Tyler approached and touched Brooke's arm. "It's time to go to James's house for the reception, Brooke," he said. "Are you ready?"

"Sure, just let me get my jacket," Brooke said. She walked toward the coatrack.

After Brooke departed, Kaylee decided this was the moment she'd been waiting for.

"Excuse me, Tyler," she said. "Could I speak with you please? In private?"

The two walked a few feet away from the remaining guests milling around.

Tyler looked at Kaylee expectantly. "Is this about the investigation? Will you be able to help?"

"Sheriff Maddox doesn't want me to."

"But he can't stop you from accepting my offer to work as a consultant."

"Perhaps not. But that's not what I want to talk to you about."

He waited impatiently, glancing occasionally at Brooke, who had reappeared with her purse and looked to be making polite conversation with Reese.

"I just wanted you to know that I gave James's watch to the sheriff. He has it as part of the evidence."

"James's watch?" His eyes narrowed in confusion. "How is that evidence?"

"James was wearing it that day. It fell from the widow's walk, and Bear, my dog, brought it to me."

"And this is important why?"

"You're James's executor, aren't you?"

"I am."

"I thought you should know about his watch. Though I'm not sure it's his."

"Sure it is. He wore it every day."

"There's an engraving on the back. It says: *To T.S.* Maybe it belongs to you."

Tyler held up his left wrist, which held a simple watch with a leather band. "This is the only one I own. As you can see, I'm wearing it."

"Then I guess T. S. doesn't stand for Tyler Stevens."

"It's not like I'm the only T. S. around here. Now if that's all, Brooke needs me."

"I just thought you should know."

"Thank you," he said dismissively, then left before Kaylee could respond. He stepped close to Brooke, said something to her in a low voice, and escorted her from the church.

After watching them go, Reese joined Kaylee. "What was that all about?"

"Only trying to satisfy my idle curiosity," she replied.

"Something to do with the investigation into James's murder?"

"Sheriff Maddox told me to leave the investigating to him."

"And that's stopping you?" He gently elbowed her. "I think I know you better than that, Kaylee Bleu."

"It's only that I think a couple of things might be important. The sheriff doesn't agree with me."

"Just promise me you'll be careful, okay? Don't keep anything from the sheriff."

"I won't."

"Good." He loosened his tie and removed his suit jacket. "Guess I've got a job to do."

"I'll help you."

"I won't say no. That was a nice thing you did for Brooke. With the lavender."

"Anybody would have done the same."

"But no one else did."

"What you're doing is nice too," Kaylee said. "Moving these flowers, I mean. I heard that Tyler Stevens arranged a catered feast at the estate for the mourners."

"My motives weren't entirely altruistic." Reese grinned sheepishly.

"Oh?"

"Big crowds like that?" He gave an exaggerated shiver. "I'd rather do this."

"Likewise."

A transformation seemed to take place as they loaded the arrangements into their vehicles. Despite their funeral attire, they'd become Kaylee and Reese to each other once again, just two friends doing what they could to help someone else.

That may be all they'd ever be. But there wasn't anything wrong with that.

"This is a stupid idea," Kaylee said to herself the next morning as she climbed into the front seat of her car and shifted into drive. After her conversation with Tyler Stevens at the funeral yesterday, however, this seemed the next logical step.

She had three good reasons to talk to Tim Slade. First, his initials were T. S. so he might be the owner of the watch. If so, he could tell her why James had it.

Second, if she found oleander on Tim Slade's property, it might help prove Brooke was innocent. Or at least give any potential jury reasonable doubt.

Third, if someone was trying to frame Brooke, then perhaps that person had bought honey identical to Brooke's from the beekeeper.

It seemed that the island's recluse might have all the answers to the mystery surrounding James's murder.

She realized she had passed the turnoff leading to the Slade property. She had to pull into a driveway farther down the road to turn around, then drive back along the road until she found it again. She turned and proceeded carefully along the rutted lane.

The modest house seemed overshadowed by a large barn badly in need of paint. Kaylee shut off her ignition and wished she had brought Bear for company. The place seemed eerily quiet.

Gathering her courage, she walked toward the rickety porch. The front door stood wide open, but Kaylee hesitated and knocked on the frame.

"Mr. Slade," she called. "Are you here?"

She strained to hear a reply, but no one answered. She took a couple steps into the foyer and called again. This time she heard a sound. Was someone crying?

She walked softly on the scarred wooden floor of the front room past piles of newspapers, assorted boxes, and gardening tools. Once inside the kitchen door, she hesitated.

A woman knelt on the dingy linoleum floor, weeping.

Kaylee started to kneel beside her, then gasped at the sight of a pudgy man sprawled near the stove. "Is that Tim Slade?"

The woman beside her sobbed an affirmative, and Kaylee really looked at her for the first time.

Oh no.

"Brooke?"

13

Kaylee swallowed hard and willed her breakfast to stay where it belonged. The man was sprawled on his back, his body perfectly still, and a bloodstained carving knife lay on the floor beside him.

"What did you do?"

Brooke's head jerked. "I didn't do anything. You have to believe me, Kaylee. I didn't kill him."

Kaylee's heart lurched in her chest. She wanted to believe Brooke, but how could she? Maybe Sheriff Maddox had been right all along. Brooke had framed herself for James's murder knowing the evidence would never stand up in court. Not as long as she had an aggressive attorney like Tyler Stevens looking out for her.

But why did she have to kill Tim Slade? Did he know something no one else did?

"Tell me you believe me," Brooke cried, her voice desperate.

"I want to," Kaylee said quietly. "But I don't know that I can."

While Brooke took deep gulping breaths, Kaylee steeled herself to close Tim Slade's unblinking eyes. She should call 911. She should move Brooke away from the scene.

But her feet, her body, seemed frozen as if she were stuck in one of her nightmares. She looked away and focused on the window opposite the stove. Sunlight filtered in through the dingy panes, a gentle reminder that goodness existed in the world despite the horrific crime that had taken place inside this house.

Brooke's breathing slowed and her weeping quieted.

Kaylee stood and pulled Brooke up with her. "Let's go outside," she said, keeping her voice as soothing as possible. "I need to call 911."

Brooke allowed herself to be led to the porch and seated on a small bench near the front window while Kaylee made the call.

"He was like that when I arrived," Brooke said when Kaylee joined her. "You have to believe me."

"Brooke, I'm not an expert, but I don't think he's been dead very long."

"But it wasn't me. I swear it wasn't."

"Please. Just start at the beginning. Why are you here?"

Brooke thrust a business card into Kaylee's hand. "I found this in my bag when I left the estate yesterday. Read it."

Kaylee examined the card. On the front was the logo for Tim Slade's beekeeping and honey operation along with his name, address, and phone number.

"Turn it over," Brooke said.

Kaylee did so and read the handwritten note:

Tomorrow at ten. Come alone.

T.S.

Next to the initials was an artistic depiction of a plant that very closely resembled an oleander.

T. S.

Tim Slade.

As Tyler had pointed out, there were others with the same initials. But how likely was it that Tim Slade, James, and the watch weren't somehow related? Especially now that both men were dead.

"Did you tell Tyler about the note? Or Kathy?" Kaylee asked.

Brooke clutched at her knees, bringing them close to her chest as if to make herself as small as possible. "I didn't tell anyone."

"Do you know for sure that Tim wrote this?"

Brooke looked at Kaylee like she was crazy. "What?"

"Is this his handwriting? Do you recognize it?"

"No," Brooke said hotly. "Why would I?"

"I don't know. I thought maybe you'd seen his handwriting at some point." Kaylee decided to take another tack. "Did you see anyone else? Pass anyone on the way here?"

"No. Did you?"

"No."

"This doesn't look too good for me, does it?"

"Tell me the truth, Brooke. Did you do it?"

Brooke stood suddenly. "It doesn't really matter, does it? James is dead and most everyone in town believes I killed him. Now Mr. Slade has been killed. You'll tell the sheriff you found me here. And because you're you, everyone will believe you're telling the truth."

"I would be telling the truth."

"So am I. But nobody wants to believe me."

"I believe you. At least . . ." Kaylee didn't finish the sentence. She hadn't believed Brooke killed James, didn't believe she was framing herself in an attempt to ward off suspicion. Based on the scene she had just encountered, however, she wasn't sure whether or not Brooke had killed Tim Slade.

"Why would I kill him?" Brooke shook her head sadly. "He was always so nice about the honey."

"Did you ever think that he might be the one who put the poison in the jar?"

"Never. He may have been a little strange, but he had a gentle heart. He didn't deserve to die like this."

"Nobody does." Kaylee stood and looked toward the inside

of the house. "I'm going to look around a little bit before anyone else arrives. Will you be all right out here by yourself?"

"Are you sure you should go in there? Couldn't you be charged with disturbing a crime scene or something like that?"

"I won't touch anything. Tyler asked me to see if there were any oleander plants around here. Remember?"

Brooke made a harrumphing noise. "Tyler was grabbing at straws. Tim didn't have anything to do with James's death. I know he didn't."

"You can't know for sure," Kaylee said.

Brooke didn't answer, but she thrust out her chin and the unexpected look of stubborn defiance on her face surprised Kaylee. This was the Brooke who had finally stood up to Alicia at The Flower Patch a couple of days ago. A Brooke made of sterner stuff than she usually let anyone see.

"I'll be back out in a minute or two," Kaylee said. "Wait for me out here."

Brooke stared out at the horizon, her eyes unreadable. But Kaylee thought she knew what she was thinking. Those who wanted to brand Brooke with a scarlet *M* for *murderer* would be even more certain of her guilt now. Kaylee could already imagine the gossip. Brooke killed James. Tim had helped her. Then Brooke killed Tim to keep him quiet.

But it was all too simple. Too straightforward. The evidence pointed too conveniently to Brooke and now here she was, conveniently near the body.

Kaylee considered all the different angles of the case as best she could while she wandered around the front room and then into the bathroom and bedroom. There were no plants anywhere in the small house. Kaylee went back to the kitchen and gingerly stepped around Tim Slade's body to reach the back porch.

Here the story was different. The enclosed porch was practically a plant nursery. Kaylee perused the row of plant stands and shelves along the wall on both sides of the door. One section was glassed to form a small greenhouse. Though fascinated by the variety, Kaylee tried not to get too sucked into identifying each individual plant but quickly checked to see if any of them could be oleanders.

None of them were.

She exited through the rear door and heard the distant sound of a motor. Initially, she thought it must be the first responders on their way to the farm, but then she noticed the noise of the engine was fading instead of getting louder.

She raced around the house to the front porch. Brooke was gone, but she'd left Tim Slade's business card behind along with another note written on a torn piece of newspaper.

> *I'm sorry, Kaylee. But I can't go to jail again, especially not for something I didn't do.*
>
> —B

Kaylee placed both hands on the porch rail, leaning her weight on them, and bowed her head. How could she have been so stupid? Sheriff Maddox would blame her for letting Brooke get away. *As well he should.* But even if she hadn't gone back into the house, she wouldn't have been able to keep Brooke from leaving. Besides, she hadn't even seen Brooke's car when she parked.

She recalled Brooke's look of determination, the set of her jaw, the hard glint in her inscrutable eyes.

No, there was nothing she could have done. But there was something she had to do—call Sheriff Maddox now and warn him that Brooke was on the run.

Kaylee opened the contacts list on her phone and found the sheriff's number. At least Brooke wouldn't get too much of a head start.

Kaylee's logical side, her forensically trained side, told her to press the call button. But her emotional side, her "want to be a good friend" side, caused her to hesitate. Despite finding Brooke crouched over Tim's body, Kaylee didn't believe she was guilty of killing him any more than she was of killing James. She'd been too distraught, and her protestations of innocence had been too sincere.

It didn't matter. She didn't want to be accused of obstructing justice.

Kaylee tapped the key connecting her to Sheriff Maddox's direct line. When the call went to voice mail, she left a message.

"It's Kaylee Bleu," she said. "I'm at Tim Slade's farm and . . . well, he's dead. I already called 911, but I wanted to let you know that Brooke was here when I got here, but she left. She's scared, and I . . . I don't know what to think. So I'll be here." She ended the call. The first responders should be here soon. Until then, there was nothing for her to do but wait.

It seemed only a few seconds later that she heard the distant sound of a siren, and soon after that a sheriff's vehicle sped up the lane, kicking up dirt and gravel. The driver parked next to Kaylee's Ford Escape, and Deputy Nick Durham climbed out from behind the wheel. At the sight of Kaylee, he removed his sunglasses and rushed toward her.

"Are you all right?" he asked. "What's going on out here?"

"Don't you know?" she asked, puzzled.

"I was already on my way here when I got the call that Slade was dead. What are you doing here?"

"I came to ask Mr. Slade about the watch. I found him and called 911."

"Stratford's watch?" He shook his head. "Never mind. That can wait. Where is Slade?"

"In the kitchen."

"Are you sure he's dead?"

"Pretty sure."

"Stay out here while I investigate. I'll be back in a few minutes."

Kaylee stood near the porch railing and rubbed her arms against a sudden chill as the blaring of more sirens grew louder and louder.

An ambulance arrived, and the driver parked close to the porch. Kaylee directed the EMTs into the house. Giles Akin, the coroner, arrived shortly after.

"We're in the midst of difficult days," he said in way of a greeting. "First James Stratford and now Timothy Slade."

"Does seem odd, doesn't it?"

"You've got to stop doing this, Kaylee."

"Doing what?"

"Discovering the dead."

"I hope it never happens again," Kaylee said. "I'd rather leave it to the professionals." She started to tell him she wasn't the one who had discovered Tim Slade lying dead in his own blood on his kitchen floor. But he was already moving toward the doorway, and she wasn't yet ready to face the questions she knew were coming. Besides, Giles wasn't the one who needed to know that Brooke had been here. She needed to tell Nick that bit of news when he came back outside. No matter how little she wanted to.

14

While she waited for Nick to return, Kaylee lowered herself to the porch bench and leaned back against the exterior wall of the house. It seemed this nightmare was never going to end.

Her mind puzzled over the strange, awkward pieces. James Stratford, the town's handsome millionaire with more enemies than friends. Tim Slade, the town's misfit recluse who kept to himself and to his bees. A watch, worn by one man but with the initials of another.

How could these pieces possibly fit together?

And how could they not?

It gave her a headache to even think about the complexities of the case. Or cases.

Could there be more than one?

Kaylee didn't think so. The men were tied to each other by Brooke and her love of honey. The woman had been engaged to one victim and discovered with the other's body shortly after his death. As much as she racked her brain, Kaylee couldn't come up with a satisfying explanation for anything that had happened in the past week.

After what felt like a very long fifteen or twenty minutes, Nick returned to the porch and sat beside Kaylee.

"I need to take your statement," he said simply.

"There's not much to tell."

"Did you think the watch we have in evidence belonged to Slade? Because of the initials?"

"I wanted to ask him."

"So you drove out here by yourself." He raised an eyebrow at her.

"Why not?" Kaylee tried to focus on the boxed beehives in the distance instead of how much she wished she was anywhere else. She had told herself that coming out here was a bad idea. If only she had listened. "He wasn't a dangerous man, was he?"

"No," Nick admitted. "Though apparently he had a dangerous enemy."

"If I'd gotten here sooner," Kaylee said softly, "maybe he'd still be alive."

Nick grunted, and she knew what he was thinking. Whoever killed the beekeeper might have killed her too in that scenario.

Kaylee cleared her throat. She couldn't put off telling him the truth any longer.

"Before you take my statement, I have to tell you . . . someone else was here when I arrived." She said the words quickly, letting them tumble over each other in a rush.

Nick's body seemed to expand like a balloon being filled with helium before he let out a forceful, "*What?*"

Kaylee quickly stood, but so did Nick. He towered over her.

"Who else was here?" he demanded.

Kaylee took a deep breath. "Brooke," she said quietly. "Brooke Edgars was here."

"Brooke." Nick practically spat her name. "Where is she now?"

"She left."

"Where did she go?"

Kaylee shrugged. "I was around back looking at the plants on the porch. I didn't know she was going to leave. I already called Sheriff Maddox."

"What did he say?"

"He didn't answer. I left a message."

Nick flipped the switch on his radio and asked the dispatcher to put out an all-points-bulletin for Brooke Edgars.

"Sheriff already did that," the dispatcher replied. "Do you know what she's driving?"

"Hang on a sec." Nick looked expectantly at Kaylee.

"I didn't see her car," she said. "But she usually drives a silver coupe."

Nick relayed the information into his radio, then stood near the porch's wooden column, one hand on the post and one on his hip. "Why did you wait so long to tell me this important piece of information, Ms. Bleu?" he asked.

Kaylee looked away, unable to meet his gaze. Naturally she didn't want anyone in the sheriff's office to doubt her professionalism.

"It never occurred to me she would leave. I was on the back porch and then I heard a car engine." She stopped and bent her head. Her explanation didn't matter. She'd let a possible murderer leave a crime scene.

"The sheriff is on his way out here," Nick said. "He'll want to talk to you, so it'd be best if you could stick around until he gets here."

Kaylee swallowed and nodded. She did not need to get herself in any more trouble with the law.

The minutes dragged by as photographs were taken, the crime scene processed, and Tim Slade's body eventually removed from the house.

Kaylee's spirits sank lower with every passing minute.

No one should have to attend her fiancé's funeral and find

another dead body in less than twenty-four hours. No wonder Brooke had broken down into a blubbering mess when she'd arrived at the house and found the reclusive beekeeper on his kitchen floor. Kaylee wouldn't mind giving in to a minor meltdown herself.

After he'd arrived on the scene, Sheriff Maddox had talked to her just long enough to sketch out a timeline of events. He had tagged the business card with the cryptic note written on the back and the note Brooke had left for Kaylee as evidence. Otherwise, he'd requested she stick around but had left her to her own devices.

She wandered out to the beehives without getting too close and then to the nearby gardens. The plants, an eclectic variety of sunflowers, marigolds, alyssum, and clover were healthy and thriving.

Sadly, Tim Slade would never again enjoy their beauty.

During her brief talk with Sheriff Maddox, Kaylee had asked about Tim's family. The sheriff had told her that the beekeeper never married, but he did have a sister who had moved to Montana about twenty years before and never returned. He had no idea whether Tim had kept in touch with her, but they'd do their best to track her down and let her know what had happened.

The trouble was, no one really knew what had happened. All they could do was speculate and theorize.

In the meantime, the only person mourning the untimely death of Tim Slade seemed to be his suspected killer—Brooke Edgars.

Out of habit, Kaylee stooped to pull a few stray weeds from the garden.

Sheriff Maddox approached, but Kaylee didn't get up. It somehow helped to steady her to be among the plants, to take away the weeds among the rich dirt.

"Any of this oleander?" Sheriff Maddox asked.

"No," Kaylee said. "I doubt Mr. Slade would grow any poisonous plants. He wouldn't have wanted the bees to use their nectar in the honey or accidentally get their pollen in it. If people had gotten sick from his honey, that probably would have been the end of his business."

Sheriff Maddox squatted on his haunches and plucked a blade of grass. He rubbed it between his fingers and gestured at the beehives. "You sure we can't pin Stratford's murder on these bees?"

"I wish it could have been that simple."

"Sheriff!" A voice called from the house drawing their attention. Nick stood on the porch and waved for them to return.

"Duty calls." The sheriff rose and offered his hand to Kaylee. "I can't tell you how glad I'll be when the most intense point of my day goes back to handing out a traffic citation or sorting out the occasional bar fight."

"We should never complain about being bored," Kaylee mused.

"Agreed."

When they neared the porch, Nick spoke. "We found something interesting under the kitchen sink."

"You go ahead," Kaylee said. "I'll wait out here."

"No can do," Nick said. "You need to see this too."

Nick headed toward the house while Kaylee exchanged glances with the sheriff. He shrugged then gestured for her to precede him through the door.

Once inside the kitchen, Kaylee tried to ignore the pooled blood and the numbered yellow signs marking where the body and the knife had been found. The cabinet doors beneath the sink stood wide open revealing an assortment of cleaning supplies, a box of trash bags, and a plant in a striped ceramic pot.

"Is this what I think it is?" Nick asked.

"*Nerium oleander*," Kaylee said, her tone resigned.

Sheriff Maddox let out a low whistle. "So what was our beekeeper doing with a poisonous plant? Specifically the kind that killed James? You just said he probably wouldn't have risked his bees collecting pollen from it and getting it in the honey."

Kaylee wished she had an answer for him. "May I?" she asked.

The sheriff arched his eyebrows at Nick.

"Already took the photos," the deputy said.

"Then go ahead, Kaylee."

"Allow me." Nick pulled the plant from beneath the sink and set it on the counter.

"The pot looks identical to the one found in Brooke's house," Kaylee said. "The plants seem to be about the same size too."

"Two poisonous plants," Nick said. "Did Tim give one to Brooke, or did Brooke give one to Tim?"

"Or maybe they came from someone else," Sheriff Maddox replied.

"Who?" Nick asked.

"I have no idea," the sheriff admitted. "But I intend to find out."

While the men talked, Kaylee studied the plant as if the answers to all their questions could be found within its splayed leaves.

"Any thoughts, Kaylee?" Sheriff Maddox asked.

"I don't think it's been under there very long," she said. "It's a healthy plant. There are no signs of distress from lack of light." She touched the soil. "It's been watered recently. I suppose Mr. Slade could have put it under the sink to hide it from someone."

"From whom?" the sheriff asked.

"The murderer?" Kaylee suggested. "Or maybe the murderer put it there?"

The sheriff's attention was called elsewhere, and Nick followed him, leaving Kaylee to study the mysterious oleander.

In all that had happened, only one new fact had emerged

from her trip to Tim Slade's house. The watch might have belonged to the beekeeper, but he wasn't the mystery runner. He was too short, too pudgy.

She gently touched the tip of one of the thick leaves. "Where did you come from?" she asked, so softly no one else could hear her. "And who put you in such a dark place?"

When Kaylee finally returned to The Flower Patch, Mary insisted on a detailed account of everything that had happened. Though she no longer worked as a police dispatcher, she remained in the loop when it came to the local law enforcement. Her husband, Herb, had dropped in to keep his wife company, and they were both aghast to hear of Tim Slade's untimely death.

"My first mail route was out that way," Herb said. He'd recently retired from the postal service. "Tim was just a kid back then."

"What happened to his family?" Kaylee asked.

"That was his uncle's place." Herb settled back in the break room's recliner and folded his hands across his paunch. "Tim's dad took off to find his fortune and married Tim's mom in Louisiana or Mississippi," he continued. "One of those states."

"Both parents died," Mary interjected. "A car accident I believe. Tim and his sister came here to live with their uncle."

"They were quiet children," Herb said. "Kept to themselves. No one was surprised when the girl took off. We all thought Tim would too."

"He was a good nephew," Mary said. "He took care of his uncle when his health failed. No one could have been more attentive. I heard he visited him practically every day when he went to live at the nursing home."

"The uncle's been gone quite a few years now," Herb added. "Without a reason to come into town, well, Tim hardly ever did. I guess he liked his own company best."

"Sounds like he's had a tough life," Kaylee said as she adjusted Bear's hunter-green bow tie.

"Definitely not an easy one," Mary said. "Has Eddie contacted the sister?"

"He probably has by now. They found an address for her in a desk drawer."

"I suppose that means we'll be busy with more orders." Mary sighed heavily. "I think we've made enough funeral arrangements in the last few days to last a lifetime."

"I agree," Kaylee said. "Though I doubt we'll have as many for Mr. Slade as we had for James."

"You're probably right." Mary's eyes slightly closed as if she were deep in thought. "But he'll have a few even if I have to order them all myself."

"Now, Mary—" Herb began.

"Never you mind saying whatever you think you want to say," Mary said. "My mind's already made up."

Kaylee smiled at their good-hearted bickering. It was so nice to escape the unpleasant events of the last week and relax with people she loved. She checked the clock on the wall and was sad to see that it was past time for her and Bear to go home. Tomorrow would be another long and difficult day. Her thoughts turned to Brooke, wondering where she had gone. She'd heard from Sheriff Maddox shortly after she arrived at the flower shop. Brooke wasn't at her house, at the Stratford estate, or with Kathy Fitz. He'd even sent Deputy Garcia to Tyler Stevens's home. But Brooke wasn't there either, and Tyler swore he hadn't heard from her.

Where else could she be?

15

The next day, Kaylee focused on cleaning and organizing the work area. With all the floral arrangements they had created in the past few hectic days, things had gotten a little out of control. She and Mary both preferred a tidy and organized space, with each ribbon, embellishment, and tool in a specific designated place.

She hadn't heard from Sheriff Maddox, so she couldn't help wondering if Brooke had been found. And what about Tim Slade's sister? How had she reacted to the news of her brother's death? What would happen to his beehives, to the Slade property?

Hopefully, James's development plans wouldn't continue. Could his management team still move forward with them? Would Mr. Slade's sister care enough about the land to stop it, or would she be grateful for the money?

Too many questions and not nearly enough answers.

She heard footsteps on the stairs and Mary entered the workroom. She handed Kaylee an envelope. "This was taped to the back door," she said. "It's addressed to you."

"That's strange," Kaylee said peering at her name scrawled on the front in an unfamiliar handwriting. She slit open the envelope and pulled out a photograph of two teenage girls posing in front of a colorful mural. The artwork included the local lighthouse, the shoreline, and a whale playing in the sea.

"This is Brooke's cousin," Kaylee said, pointing to one of the girls. "I recognize her from the photograph I found on the beach."

Mary slipped on her glasses before taking the photograph to get a better look. "The other girl isn't Brooke, though."

"No." Kaylee looked inside the envelope but it was empty. "No note."

Mary turned the photograph over. "I thought you said this was Brooke's cousin."

"I did."

"I don't think so."

Kaylee peered over Mary's shoulder and read the inscription out loud. "Brooke Edgars and Alicia Wellington-Simms, participants."

Puzzled, Kaylee took the photograph again and studied the two young girls. "So this is Alicia," she said more to herself than to Mary. "But this should be Beth, not Brooke."

"Maybe whoever wrote that made a mistake," Mary said. "After all, this picture was taken at least ten or fifteen years ago, and the cousins looked very much alike. I mean, couldn't that be Brooke?"

"I suppose. Brooke told me their mothers were twins." She turned over the photograph. "This writing isn't recent. See how the ink has faded."

Mary examined the inscription then the writing on the envelope. "You're right about the ink," she said. "Do you think this is the same handwriting?"

Kaylee compared the writing then shook her head. "I'm not sure. My name looks like it was written by someone trying to disguise their writing. But why send me this photo in the first place?"

"I suppose it could have something to do with James's death," Mary said. "I don't know how the two things could be connected, though."

"It's Brooke," Kaylee said. "She's the only one connected to everything else—to James, to Mr. Slade, to these photographs."

"And she's disappeared."

"No one will ever believe she's innocent now."

"Except you," Mary said laying a comforting hand on Kaylee's arm.

"Even I'm beginning to have my doubts." She studied the photograph again.

"I remember when those murals were created," Mary said. "I don't mean the exact year. But it was one of those competitions sponsored by Art Attack to rev up community spirit, when Nora Keller's aunt still owned the store. This was before they started doing the talent shows."

"Sounds like they were fun."

"Most of the stores along Market Boulevard participated," Mary continued, "especially the ones south of Main Street and across from Sculpture Park. Different teams of artists, including selected students, got to paint a mural on the sides of the buildings. From this photo, I'd say Alicia and whoever this is were partners."

"They don't look particularly happy, do they?" Kaylee mused.

"The murals were judged. Maybe they didn't win."

"Maybe." Kaylee placed the photograph on the table. She retrieved her phone and found the picture she'd taken of the photograph pieces she'd found on the beach. The girl who wasn't Alicia in the mural photograph was definitely the same girl she'd identified as Beth in the torn photograph.

"Since I can't ask Brooke about this photo," Kaylee said, "I'll have to ask the next best person."

"Alicia?"

"She's the next worst person. I was thinking Jessica." Kaylee put the photo back in the envelope. "I won't be gone long."

"Take your time," Mary said. "I'm going to start on a special design for Tim Slade's funeral."

Kaylee waved to Jessica as she entered the Death by Chocolate bakery and coffee shop, conveniently located next door to The

Flower Patch. Jessica returned the greeting and turned back to the customer she was helping. Kaylee loitered by the counter, inspecting Oliver, Jessica's prized lavender geranium.

"He doesn't look good, does he?" Jessica asked as she joined Kaylee. "Too much grief and mourning on the island for him to be at his best." One of Jessica's lovable quirks was her reliance on Oliver as a forecaster of doom and gloom. The plant did appear droopy, and several petals carpeted the soil beneath the leaves.

"Have you heard anything about Brooke?" Kaylee asked.

"Not a word." Jessica sighed. "Can I get you something? Iced tea? Blackberry lemonade? I'm thinking of having one myself."

"Only if you're having some too. I just stopped in to show you something that was left for me at the shop." Kaylee handed the photograph to Jessica.

Jessica studied the image. "This takes me back. I remember how disappointed Mila was that she didn't get to paint any of the murals. They were painted right there on the storefronts for everyone to see, so only the best art students were selected. Mila has a lot of talents, but painting isn't one of them." Jessica handed the photo back to Kaylee, then reached for a pitcher of lemonade and two glasses.

"I'm sure that kind of rejection would be hard for a teenage girl to take," Kaylee said.

Jessica chuckled as she poured lemonade over crushed ice. "Probably just as well. These two," she said gesturing toward the photo, "had a horrible argument when their mural didn't win. They barely spoke to each other after that, and they wanted Mila to take sides. Mila didn't care too much for Alicia anyway, but it was still hard for her. Then Brooke moved away, so that put an end to the spats."

"You mean Beth moved away?"

"They left at the same time. After their grandmother died, they moved to Missouri to live with a distant relative. An aunt, I think, but it's been so long ago, I don't really remember."

"But this is Beth in the photo. Right?"

Jessica looked at Kaylee in confusion. "The girls were practically twins, but I'm fairly certain this is Brooke." She took the photo and examined it again. "Her hair is darker than Beth's and her face is slightly rounder."

Kaylee brought up the photo on her phone of the torn photograph and pointed to each girl as she said their names. "But I thought this was Brooke and this was Beth. That's what you said."

Jessica stared at her and laughed. "This is Brooke," she said pointing to the girl Kaylee thought was Beth. "And *this* is Beth. I think we got our signals crossed."

Kaylee laughed too. "I guess we did. They look so much alike here. Our Brooke looks just the way I would predict young Beth to look when she grew up." Then she compared the photographs again. "So Brooke and Alicia had this huge fight but never made up."

"You know how kids are. They let molehills become mountains."

"Do you think it's strange, given their history, that Brooke would hire Alicia to be her wedding planner?"

"I think anyone, especially Alicia, would have seen it as a major betrayal if James and Brooke had chosen anyone else. And this all happened a long time ago. I'm sure sometime in the years between then and now, they forgot all about their childhood rivalry."

"Someone hasn't forgotten."

"Who's that?"

"Whoever taped this photo to my door."

The shop door opened and a customer entered the bakery, so Kaylee took a seat at one of the café tables while Jessica boxed a selection of miniature cupcakes.

A few minutes later, Jessica set down a double fudge brownie with two forks in front of Kaylee and took a seat across from her.

Kaylee looked up from her phone. "I feel so foolish," she said. She held up her screen, which displayed an image of the torn photo she'd found on the beach. "Both you and Brooke told me who was in this photograph, so why did I get the two girls mixed up?"

"Don't be so hard on yourself. It's really kind of funny, don't you think?"

"I suppose so," Kaylee said, a little uneasy. It was so unlike her to get that confused. She handed the envelope to Jessica. "I don't suppose you recognize the handwriting."

"Can't say that I do."

"It could have been anybody. But what does it mean?"

"Are you going to tell Sheriff Maddox about this photo?" Jessica asked, pointing to the one of Brooke and Alicia.

"He didn't seem to think the first one mattered all that much."

"But someone wanted you to see this one. I wonder why."

"I have no idea. But to answer your question, yes. I'll tell the sheriff about it."

The ringtone of Kaylee's phone interrupted their conversation. The number was local but not one she recognized. She answered the call. "Kaylee Bleu."

"Hi, Kaylee. This is Kathy Fitz."

The librarian?

"Hi, Kathy. What can I do for you?"

"I know this sounds odd, but I wondered if I could talk to you for a few minutes. In person."

"Sure. I'm next door at the bakery but—"

"Could we make it someplace more private? Perhaps at Wildflower Cottage?"

Kaylee frowned. "What's this all about?"

"I'd rather not say over the phone." Kathy paused. "I wouldn't ask if it weren't important."

"I can be there in about fifteen or twenty minutes."

"Thanks, Kaylee. I appreciate this."

The call ended, and Kaylee gazed at Jessica. "Kathy Fitz wants to come out to my place."

"Did she say why?"

"I can guess."

"Me too."

"Brooke," they said simultaneously.

Kaylee stuffed the photograph back into the envelope. "I need to ask Mary to stay late again. I hope she won't mind."

"Wait," Jessica said. "You can't go without me."

"What about the bakery?"

"Gretchen is in the back making truffles. I'll go tell her to listen for customers." Jessica flashed a bright smile. "And I'll grab some snacks for us while I'm at it."

Kaylee chuckled, thankful once again for her friend's irrepressible spirit. "Okay, I'll meet you out at the cottage soon."

Kaylee arrived at Wildflower Cottage only a few minutes before Jessica. She immediately put the tea kettle on the stove and set out cups and saucers.

Jessica brought in a box of chocolate goodies and set to work arranging them on a translucent green plate. "This is one of my favorite patterns," she said. "Doric, isn't it?"

"I think so. Grandma left me several pieces from her Depression glass collection. That's one of my favorites too." Kaylee placed folded napkins on the kitchen island. "Where do you think we should meet with Kathy?"

"I think we want someplace informal," Jessica said. "I don't know about you, but I'm so keyed up I feel like I'm about to pop."

"Let's take these things to the sunroom. At least then we'll have a view of the meadow. It could be calming."

"Do you think Kathy knows where Brooke is?"

"I think she knows something else." Unable to predict why Kathy wanted to see her, Kaylee had focused her thoughts on the photographs during the drive to Wildflower Cottage. As she relived her conversation with Brooke, she realized why she had gotten the two girls mixed up in the torn photograph.

Because of Brooke.

And Kaylee could think of only one reason why Brooke would have purposely confused her as to their identities. Then when she showed the photograph to Jessica, neither Kaylee nor Jessica had specified which girl was which. Jessica had known who was who, but Kaylee had assumed she knew who was who too.

She'd have continued mixing them up if not for the mysterious photograph that had been taped to her back door.

Someone wanted her to be aware of her mistake. And she believed she knew who that someone was. Now she just needed to find out why.

Kaylee heard tires crunch on the gravel drive, and Bear let out an alert bark and scampered toward the front door. She peered out the kitchen window as Kathy parked her vehicle behind the Ford Escape.

"She's here," Kaylee told Jessica. She stayed by the window as Kathy stepped out of the car and scanned the property. Then she motioned and someone emerged from the other side. Kaylee's jaw dropped as she recognized Kathy's companion.

"Brooke's here too." Kaylee grimaced and made a quick decision. She owed it to Brooke to at least hear her out. "We can't go to the sunroom. It's too open."

"You go to the door," Jessica said. "I'll move the refreshments to the dining room."

Kaylee nodded and hurried toward the foyer. She opened the door before Kathy and Brooke had climbed the steps to the porch. "Come in," she said as she scanned the street for any unfamiliar cars or anything that looked out of place.

Once the door was shut behind them, Kaylee embraced Brooke. "Are you all right? I've been so worried."

"I'm fine," Brooke said. "Are you sure you don't mind me being here? You could be charged with harboring a fugitive."

"I'll face that if and when it happens." Kaylee turned to Kathy. "Jessica Roberts is here."

Kathy grabbed Brooke's arm. "Maybe we should go."

"You can trust her," Kaylee said. "As much as you trust me."

Brooke nodded and smiled at Kathy. "Her daughter and I were good friends when we were kids. It's fine."

"I hope you're right," Kathy said. She faced Kaylee. "It's not a matter of trust. I know Jessica is a good and honest person. But in a situation like this—"

"Please don't worry," Jessica said as she entered from the kitchen and took Brooke's hands in hers. She studied the young woman's features. "I won't judge you," she said. "But I think it's time you told us the truth."

"You know?" Brooke asked, her voice suddenly small and tense.

"Not until this very moment," Jessica answered. "I should have seen it before, I suppose."

"We tried hard to make sure nobody would," Kathy said.

Kaylee locked the door and gestured toward the hallway. "Jessica set up some snacks in the dining room."

"Thank you for letting us come here, Kaylee," Brooke said. "And for giving me a chance to explain."

"You're welcome." Kaylee smiled, the realization that had started to gel taking form at last. "Beth."

"You've guessed my secret too."

"Only because I am finally seeing it clearly. And someone gave me a nudge."

The younger woman's features tensed. "Who?"

"I had hoped it was you." Kaylee smiled warmly in hopes of easing everybody's nerves. "Let's get settled and then we can talk."

Kaylee followed the other women into the dining room and they took seats at one end of the large oak table.

"Shall I pour the tea?" Jessica asked.

Kaylee nodded and silently thanked her for adding a touch of normalcy to this odd situation. Though she had begun to suspect the truth about Brooke being Beth as she drove home from The Flower Patch, the revelation still needed to sink in. Jessica seemed to be taking the news in stride, but Kaylee felt a little at sea.

Jessica handed Brooke—no, this was Beth—a cup, and her eyes twinkled with gentle humor. "As I recall, you don't share your cousin's love for honey."

The young woman flushed and her smile seemed forced. "I hate the stuff."

"Yet all this time you've been drinking it," Jessica said. "No wonder we all thought you were Brooke."

"Please. You must still think of me as Brooke." She bit her lower lip, and Kaylee thought she was going to burst into tears. Instead her chin trembled and her eyes took on a faraway look. "I didn't drink it as much as anyone thought. James did it for me."

"He knew the truth?" Kaylee asked.

"And so did Kathy." Brooke smiled warmly at the librarian. "They kept my secret."

"But why?" Jessica asked. "You would have been as welcome in Turtle Cove as Beth as you were as Brooke."

"I'm sure that's true," Brooke said. "I must admit, I was overwhelmed by how so many people were glad I'd returned. I almost felt like a prodigal child, except I hadn't squandered any inheritance or sunk quite as low as the son in the story."

She took a sip of her tea as if to compose herself. No one spoke while she gathered her thoughts.

"I didn't come back here purposely to deceive anyone," she finally said. "Least of all you, Mrs. Roberts. You were always so kind to my cousin and to me. But I needed to deceive someone else, a guy I met after college. I thought he loved me. It turned out he had a different definition of love than I did."

"When I think about what that scumbag did to her, it makes me queasy," Kathy said, her jaw set and her fists clenched. "Restraining orders didn't keep him away. She moved a couple of times, but he always found a way to track her down."

Brooke involuntarily shivered, and her teacup rattled against the saucer as she set it down. She put her hands in her lap, her shoulders hunched as if she was trying to make her body smaller. Kaylee's heart ached to think how terrified she must have been. Her friends on the Seattle police force had once talked about a couple of abuse and stalking cases they had worked. The stories were heartbreaking and senseless. It hurt to think that this young woman had endured that kind of pain and fear.

"So you came here," Jessica said. "You came home."

"Not quite." Brooke took a couple of deep breaths as if to prepare herself for what she was about to say. "My cousin and I were living in different states after college. When I finally told her what my ex-boyfriend was doing, she wanted me to live with her. I was so afraid of putting her in danger that I ended all contact with her instead. A little over a year ago, a private detective found me. My cousin hired him because she was sick. Terminal." Brooke's voice choked. "She'd moved to Los Angeles, and he escorted me to her home. Once I was there, she told me her plan."

"They swapped identities." As Kathy spoke, she referred to the girls by their true names. "It was Brooke's last gift to her beloved cousin. Somehow, she took care of everything. When the stalker tracked Beth again, he found her name on a marker in a cemetery."

What a beautiful thing to do, to ensure that her cousin would be able to have a better life when she was gone. A tear dampened Kaylee's cheek and Jessica sniffed. Kaylee immediately rose, found a box of tissues, and set it on the table beside the teapot.

"Is that when you returned here?" Jessica asked.

"After my cousin died, I moved to Helena, Montana. That's when I started my new life as Brooke Edgars. Fortunately, we were so much alike in our interests as well as our appearance that even our college degrees were similar. My cousin majored in fashion design and I majored in interior design. I was almost surprised by how easy it was to be Brooke."

She paused, but no one rushed in to fill the silence. After a moment or two, her features relaxed into a small smile. "I was at a local coffee shop when someone tapped me on the shoulder."

"That would be me," Kathy said. "I was in Helena for the National Librarian Association conference. I knew I had just run into one of the look-alike cousins, but I didn't know which."

"At first I panicked." Brooke giggled sheepishly. "Then I realized this was a major test. If Kathy, someone I had spent a lot of time with as a child, didn't know I was lying, maybe no one else would ever know either."

"When did you figure out the truth, Kathy?" Jessica asked.

"It was the honeyed tea that tripped her up. Or the lack of it."

"We got to talking," Brooke said. "I realized how homesick I was for Turtle Cove. The more Kathy told me about the people I had once known and how few changes had taken place, the more I wanted to come back. Somehow it seemed like this was the only true home I'd ever had—where my cousin and I had been the happiest. But, of course, I didn't think I could. I'd be too easy to find here."

"Then on the last day of the conference, we went to lunch," Kathy said. "Brooke here ordered iced tea and I jokingly told the waitress to bring a jar of honey. Brooke made a face and said 'no thanks.'"

"I immediately realized I had slipped up," Brooke added. "And the truth came spilling out. I'd been holding it in so long, even the grief I'd been feeling, and Kathy was such a good listener. We stayed in touch, and when the place where I worked closed up, she persuaded me to come home."

Kaylee glanced at Kathy, who was watching Brooke with a maternal glow on her face. Kathy's own story was no secret to the residents of Turtle Cove. She'd turned down two or three marriage proposals, determined to wait for the deepest kind of love before giving up her independence. She was almost thirty when Prince Charming had come into her life. They married after a whirlwind courtship, but split up only two years later. Her prince had turned out to be a toad. Kathy had never trusted her heart again, but she'd been a shoulder for more than one young woman whose heart was broken.

"We're glad you came back, Brooke," Jessica said. "You belong here."

Brooke gazed at her own hands. "Someone in Turtle Cove doesn't agree with that." She looked up. "Why would anyone do this to me? To James?"

No one answered.

One week. Two murders.

Would there be another victim?

What if the murderer went after Brooke next?

16

After the startling story was retold, each of the women had seemed to need a break. Jessica—ever the hostess no matter where she was—had put the tea kettle back on the stove and was trying to concoct a meal out of whatever she could find in Kaylee's pantry and refrigerator. No one seemed to be hungry, but it was something to do while they processed what they'd learned.

Kaylee went outside with Bear for his last run of the night. The little dog sniffed beneath the grass on the edge of the meadow, then followed his nose on a secret expedition around the corner of the cottage. Hopefully, the trail belonged to a squirrel and not a raccoon or some type of weasel. The island's wildlife was part of its appeal, but Kaylee didn't want Bear's take-no-prisoners bravado to get him into a scrape he couldn't get out of.

She sat on the porch step and called his name. The dachshund came scurrying back around the corner and climbed into her lap. "Did you hear Brooke's story?" she asked him. *No, not Brooke. Beth. Except now she is Brooke.* Kaylee rubbed Bear's silky ears. "It makes my head spin."

So many questions still tugged at Kaylee's mind, but the two primary ones had to do with the watch and the photograph that had been delivered to her. Somehow they were related to everything else. But how?

When she returned to the house with Bear, Jessica stood at the stove whipping up omelets while Kathy cleaned fresh veggies.

Kathy smiled apologetically at Kaylee. "Brooke and I didn't mean to invite ourselves over for supper. She's in the bathroom trying to hide the dark circles under her eyes."

"Poor girl," Kaylee said. "I'm glad you brought her here." She took a stack of plates from the cupboard and set them near Kathy. "Do you mind if I ask you something?"

"You want to know where Brooke was hiding last night?"

"Well, yes. But that's not what I was going to ask."

"What is it?"

"Do you always call her Brooke instead of Beth?"

"Always," Kathy said firmly. "That's who she is now and that's how you need to think of her too. Her stalker is unstable and obsessed. The private detective who helped Brooke—helped her to become Brooke that is—sent her photographs of the guy placing flowers at 'Beth's' grave." Kathy used her fingers to make air quotes when she said the name. "She can never go back to being Beth."

"It must have been difficult for Brooke's friends. I mean the real Brooke. Didn't they wonder about where she had gone? Especially when she'd been so sick."

"She hadn't lived in Los Angeles long," Kathy said. "She'd gone there to take part in an experimental therapy. Her close friends know that she died, but they were told she was cremated. No one who knew Brooke will be looking for her grave."

"That's very sad for her." Jessica's voice slightly wavered. "And for Beth."

"I didn't want to do it," the new Brooke said. She had entered the kitchen without anyone noticing. "Not at first. But Bee had made up her mind. It was the only way to protect me. In a way, it really was me who died instead. I am Brooke. I have to be."

"Bee?" Kaylee asked.

"Your grandmother was the first to call her that." For the first time that evening, Brooke appeared to relax as she remembered her childhood days. "It was a strange kind of joke. A lot of the grown-ups who didn't know us well never bothered to learn which of us was which. So sometimes we traded places to fool them. But we could never fool Miss Bea. We'd try, and she'd pretend not to know the difference even though she always did. Brooke was Bee and I was Bop because I was always dancing around." She paused.

The room was silent as the women waited for Brooke to continue.

"And then she'd give us a carnation or a sprig of baby's breath. 'We're the three B's,' she'd say, 'and we need to stick together.' The nickname kind of stuck, at least between my cousin and me. I mean, it made sense, didn't it? Especially with how much Bee loved her honey."

"That sounds like Grandma," Kaylee said. "No one could get much past her. It's too bad she's still on her cruise. I think we could use her wisdom right now."

"I wish she was here too," Brooke said. "She'd know I didn't do what they say I did."

"We know that," Kathy said. "We're here for you, Brooke. We're going to help you."

Kaylee nodded. "Kathy's right. I don't know how, but we're going to find out who's behind these murders."

"Thank you," Brooke said. "In the past few days, I've wondered if I was wrong to come back here. But then I wouldn't have fallen in love with James, which is something I never expected to happen. And I wouldn't give it up for anything."

"Were you close as children?" Kaylee asked.

"Not at all." Brooke seemed lost in memory, and her mouth curved in a soft smile. "He had renovated a couple of properties on the other side of the island. Tyler recommended me to do the staging. From the moment we met, it was like we both knew. We were meant to be together. It may sound silly and hopelessly trite, but it's true."

Brooke looked at each of them in turn. "I know what you're

thinking," she said. "But it wasn't serious between Tyler and me. We weren't a good match, and I was about to break it off with him before all this happened with James."

Her voice caught and she plucked a tissue from the box. "Sometimes I wonder if maybe, if perhaps losing James was somehow my punishment for taking Bee's identity."

"Never think that," Jessica said. "You're doing what your cousin—what Bee—wanted you to do. You've done nothing wrong."

Brooke blinked back tears and cleared her throat. "I hate that all of this has happened. But I've never had anyone care for me the way all of you do. Not since I moved from here after my Nana died. I don't want to have to leave again."

"You won't," Jessica said firmly, though tears shimmered in her eyes too. "No more of this sniffling or the omelets will get cold. Grab your plates, ladies."

Once they were settled again at the dining room table, Kaylee handed Brooke the photograph of her cousin with Alicia. "This was left at my shop today. Do you recognize it?"

Brooke studied the photograph and a sly smile tugged at her lips. "You bet I do. I don't think I've ever seen Bee so mad."

"What happened?" Jessica asked.

"When they didn't win for their age division, Alicia threw a full-on tantrum. Bee was upset too, particularly since Alicia had refused to listen to any of her suggestions. Even their art teacher preferred Bee's ideas when he had reviewed their sketches. Alicia insisted on using her own designs. In case you haven't noticed, she usually gets what she wants."

Brooke handed the photo to Kathy so she could see it. "Alicia accused Bee of purposely doing less than her best so they wouldn't win, of purposely sabotaging their mural. Then one of the judges complimented them on the detail on the mural's lighthouse and said it was too bad the other elements hadn't been done that well. That's when Alicia really saw red. The lighthouse was the only thing she had let Bee paint."

"Looks like all has been forgiven," Jessica said. "I mean, Alicia seemed to at least act professionally for the wedding planning."

"Yes, she was gracious." Brooke shrugged. "Or as gracious as Alicia gets."

"I've seen it before," Kathy said. "Young teens who moved in completely different high school circles often become good friends as adults. Alicia hasn't outgrown her bossiness, but she's a very accomplished and creative woman. No one could have done more."

"I would have been happy with a small wedding," Brooke said. "But it just wasn't possible given all of James's connections. He hired Alicia to take the stress from me. That's the way he was, always looking out for me. I couldn't have asked for a more considerate, more loving . . ." Her voice trailed off.

"He knew about your cousin?" Kaylee asked quietly.

"Shortly after we got together, I told him everything. It wasn't even a question—I knew he'd have my back. And he did what needed to be done to help me keep up the charade, even drinking that awful honeyed tea."

"Seems like you could have just said you no longer liked it," Jessica said.

"Except it was the very thing that tripped me up with Kathy. Since she had remembered it after all these years, I figured other people would too. And they did. It was the one thing that seemed to cement into everyone's mind that I truly was Brooke."

"Are you really allergic to cats?" Kaylee asked.

"Why do you ask?" Brooke asked in surprise, then her features relaxed. "Dr. Melody. I knew I should have taken that kitten no matter how much sneezing I'd have to endure. But it was too late. I'd already told her about my allergies."

"What's this?" Jessica asked.

Kaylee told them about her conversation with Dr. Melody. "She doesn't suspect anything though."

"I'm glad," Brooke said. "They say it's the little things that always trip you up."

"Like maybe this photograph," Kaylee said, tapping the picture Brooke still held in her hands. "Do you know who took it or who put it on my door?"

"It wasn't me," Brooke said. "I wonder if Teddy took it. When he was a kid, he took a lot of pictures for the school newspaper and the yearbook. I got to thinking about that torn photograph you showed me the other day, Kaylee. I wonder if he took that too."

"Teddy who?" Kaylee asked.

"Teddy Saunders." Brooke made a face. "I forgot. He goes by Rick now. I guess he thought Rick sounded more professional than Teddy."

"Rick Saunders's name is really Teddy?" Kaylee's tone was incredulous.

"Actually it's Tedrick," Kathy said. "Odd name, isn't it? I think it may have been his mother's maiden name. Or perhaps his grandmother's. I remember it from his library card when I still worked in the school system."

"Tedrick Saunders," Kaylee said, more to herself than to the others. "T.S." Her pulse quickened as she considered Rick's height and build. He could easily have been the mystery runner. If he was the one who'd taken these photographs all those years ago, he could also be the one who threw the torn photograph on the beach and who had delivered the second photograph to The Flower Patch.

But why?

Brooke eyed Kaylee closely. "Do you think Teddy—Rick—is involved with James's murder?"

"Perhaps we should call Sheriff Maddox," Jessica suggested. "He could talk to Rick. See if he knows anything about this photo."

Brooke's face immediately lost all color. "Please don't call the sheriff," she said. "I can't go back to jail. I just can't. I didn't kill James, and I didn't kill Tim Slade." Her voice was broken by gasps and then hiccups.

Kathy immediately went to Brooke and wrapped her arms around her. "You're not going back there," she said, then looked pleadingly at Kaylee and Jessica. "I've been a law-abiding member of this community all my life. Until now. I know Brooke hasn't done anything wrong, and she's been through too much already."

"I won't call him. Not tonight anyway," Kaylee said. "Tomorrow morning I'll talk to Rick, but then I'll have to call Sheriff Maddox."

"I can live with that," Brooke said. "Thank you."

"I hate to eat and run," Kathy said. "But perhaps we should be leaving now."

"Is Brooke staying with you?" Jessica asked.

"Not exactly," Kathy said. She held up a hand when Kaylee opened her mouth. "But I think it's better if I don't say any more about that for now."

"We understand," Kaylee said. "I'll walk you out."

The women exchanged goodbyes and hugs, and then Kaylee and Jessica stood on the covered front porch as Kathy and Brooke drove away.

While gazing after the taillights, Kaylee wondered where Kathy and Brooke planned to stop next. And how difficult the road ahead was going to be for the grieving bride-to-be who'd lost everything—including her own identity.

17

The early morning sun was shining brightly when Kaylee arrived at The Flower Patch the next morning. The work area was neat and tidy, so she looked over the day's orders and checked the current inventory. After Mary arrived, Kaylee intended to walk over to Rick's studio to ask him about the second photograph and the engraved watch—even though she still had no idea how either item could be the key to solving James's murder or Tim Slade's.

Who could have benefited from the death of both men? Was it the same murderer, or was it all a coincidence? And what about Brooke's former stalker? Had he found out she was still alive? Could he be the one behind the two deaths? Perhaps he saw James as a rival and wanted him out of the way. But why kill the beekeeper?

Or maybe the murder had nothing to do with Brooke at all. Perhaps the key to solving the mystery was the dispute the two men were having over the property. In that case, the watch and the photographs were only red herrings.

Or maybe Kaylee had been reading too many of DeeDee's mystery novels.

Kaylee wandered into the flower shop's kitchen area to make a cup of coffee and gasped. Brooke sat in a chair at the table, one leg tucked beneath her as she doodled on a notepad.

Kaylee placed her hand on her heart, willing it to return to a normal pace. "How did you get in here?"

At least Brooke had the grace to look contrite as she held up a key. "I'm sorry, Kaylee. Honest I am. But this was the safest place I knew to stay."

Stunned at seeing Brooke with a key, Kaylee made coffee to calm her nerves, her mind whirling the whole time.

Bea had meant to change the locks before Kaylee took over the shop, but that item had dropped to a low priority on both her and Kaylee's to-do lists, especially with everything else they needed to accomplish to prepare for her grandmother's move to Arizona.

Now it was back to first place.

Once the water began filtering through the coffee maker, Kaylee turned to Brooke. She forced herself to speak calmly though her stomach still had butterflies from the shock. "Why do you have a key to this place?"

"Your grandmother gave it to Bee."

"Why would she do that?"

"Bee loved this house. She used to make up stories about the people who might have lived here. Or maybe the stories were about her living here. All these rooms and their nooks and crannies."

"That doesn't explain why she had a key."

"She hid out here sometimes in one of the upper rooms. We were good kids, and our grandmother loved us dearly. But she could be ultrastrict sometimes, and Bee especially needed a refuge."

"Grandma allowed that?"

Brooke nodded. "You knew her better than anyone. She always wanted to help anyone in trouble. I hoped she wouldn't mind if I hid out here too, now that I need a refuge."

"I don't know what she'd think," Kaylee said. "I'm not even sure what I think."

"I promise I didn't bother anything."

"Does Kathy know this is where you're staying?"

"I didn't want anyone to know. That way no one has to lie for me."

"That doesn't mean I won't get in trouble. If Sheriff Maddox finds out you're here—"

"I'll tell him you didn't know. And that's the truth, so what can he do?"

Put me in the jail cell next to you. The thought made Kaylee shudder. "Well, that was the truth until two minutes ago."

"I won't stay here again," Brooke said. "If I'd had any other options, I wouldn't have been here last night. You and Mrs. Roberts and Ms. Fitz have been so kind to me, done so much."

"I haven't done anything."

"You believed in me. You have no idea how much that means. It's . . ." Brooke took a moment to search for the right word. "It's everything."

Kaylee sighed in exasperation. What could she do? Brooke had already spent the night—more than once, from the sounds of it. If it became an issue, Sheriff Maddox would have to take her word for it that she didn't know about the key. She figured she ought to have Reese install new locks when he came around for the spruce-up he'd mentioned.

Until then, she might as well be as helpful, as hospitable, as she could be.

"Are you hungry?" she asked. "There's not much here to eat, but we usually have something in the fridge."

"I want to go with you to talk to Rick," Brooke said as if she hadn't heard.

"Are you sure that's wise?"

"I've thought about it all night. He's the only one who would have saved those photographs all these years. I want to know what he's doing with them now. And I want to hear it from him, not secondhand."

"Can't blame you for that," Kaylee said. In Brooke's shoes, she'd want the same thing. "As soon as Mary arrives, we can go."

Granted, they'd be taking the SUV instead of the leisurely walk Kaylee originally planned. No one else needed to know Brooke's whereabouts.

"Why don't you go wait in my car so Mary doesn't see you? It's the red Ford Escape parked out back. It's unlocked."

Brooke nodded and slipped out the door quietly.

Mary bustled into the shop a few minutes later. After a brief greeting and a selective explanation of her errand, Kaylee left The Flower Patch and joined Brooke in the car.

They were silent on the short drive to Rick's gallery. After Kaylee parked the SUV, she and Brooke hurried up the steps and slipped inside. He wasn't in the showroom, so Brooke headed straight down the hall. Kaylee hurried after her.

Rick stepped from a side room into the hallway, then halted in surprise when he saw them.

"Well, hello," he said. "What are the two of you doing here?"

"I have another photograph to show you," Kaylee said.

"In private," Brooke added.

"Naturally." Rick gestured toward the room he'd been in. "After you."

Bookcases, filing cabinets, and shelves filled the small room. Framed canvases and photographic prints leaned against the furniture, and several photo albums were awkwardly piled on a worktable. A desk, holding a laptop, a neat rack of folders, and a few other odds and ends stood in the corner. This was obviously a combination archives room and office.

Kaylee and Beth seated themselves on stools at the table while Rick pressed his palms upon its surface and gazed at Kaylee.

"I told you Brooke didn't kill James," he said. Kaylee thought she noticed a subtle emphasis on the first name. "But you should be careful who you spend your time with. I'm not so sure Beth here isn't the murderer."

"I didn't kill him," Brooke said. "I loved him." The use of the past tense seemed to pain her. "I still love him."

"I believed it," Rick said. "The way you looked at him. The way he looked at you."

"How did you know?" Kaylee asked. "About Brooke and Beth, I mean."

"I'm an artist. I have an eye for detail."

"He took several photographs of me for the portrait," Brooke explained to Kaylee. She pressed the heels of her hands against her forehead. "I was afraid that would come back to haunt me."

A tiny lightbulb came to life in Kaylee's mind. "And then you looked through your archives," she said.

Rick nodded then stared at Brooke. "The resemblance is striking," he said. "I'm not surprised you got away with it."

"She's not trying to get away with anything," Kaylee said defensively.

"Isn't she?" Rick snorted, focusing his blistering gaze on Kaylee then back to Brooke. "Where is your doppelganger?"

"She died," Brooke said. "But before she did, she gave me her name."

"James knew about this?"

"He did."

"No wonder he . . ."

"He what?" Kaylee asked. When Rick didn't reply, she pressed on, hedging bets that her hunch was right. "'To T. S. Dare and Endure.' T. S. stands for Tedrick Saunders, doesn't it? The watch belongs to you."

He stiffened but still didn't speak.

"You were the person I saw running away from the lighthouse. You tore up the photograph of Brooke and her cousin."

"I'm guessing you also saw my photograph of Brooke, the real Brooke, and Alicia," he said, his voice full of condescension.

"You weren't exactly quick on the uptake, so I thought I'd help you connect the dots. Then I wouldn't be the only one in town who knew this one's . . ." he pointed to Brooke . . . "dirty secret."

"Why did you kill James?" Brooke asked.

Rick stared at her again and anger darkened his expression. "Kill James? That wasn't me."

"I think it was," Brooke said. "You killed him and tried to frame me."

Rick shifted his gaze to Kaylee. "Is that what you think?"

She studied him, her mind going over the facts they knew and the questions that still had no answers.

"I think you were with James on the widow's walk," she said finally. "But I don't believe you killed him."

He slowly nodded and the anger faded from his eyes. "You're right. I was there. But I didn't put the poison in that mug. And I didn't want him dead. I only wanted my watch back."

"You tried to blackmail him by threatening to expose his fiancée's secret?" Kaylee asked.

"That's an ugly word. I wanted to get back something that belonged to me."

"I don't understand," Brooke said. "Why did James have your watch in the first place?"

After a heavy sigh, Rick ran both of his hands through his hair as if to pull himself together, then straightened. "I guess it doesn't matter now. It's all bound to come out."

"It's confidential?" Kaylee asked.

"No," Rick said slowly. "Only a blow to my pride."

"Tell us," Kaylee urged softly.

"The watch was a gift from a mentor I had in college. Money was tight when I was first trying to get my studio going, so I said yes when a friend—doesn't matter who—invited me to a poker game. I'm decent at reading the other players' tells. Things were going well, I was feeling good. Celebrated a little too early and a little too much. Next thing I knew, I'd lost everything I'd won. I was desperate. I had a pretty good hand, but no more money. I threw the watch in the pot."

"James won it," Brooke said.

"I accused him of cheating. Made a few threats. Enough that he refused to let me buy back the watch. Every time I saw him wearing it, I wanted to punch him out."

"So instead you tried to blackmail him," Kaylee said.

"When I suspected Brooke here wasn't who she claimed to be, I asked him to meet me. We set the time and place. I showed him the photograph, told him I knew his bride was really Brooke's cousin and not Brooke herself. I told him if he gave back the watch, I wouldn't tell anyone."

"What did he say?" Brooke asked, her eyes shiny with tears.

Kaylee could only imagine it must be hard for Brooke to hear about the man she loved acting like such a jerk. Granted, Rick wasn't the only person in Turtle Cove who felt that way about James. How one person could secure the affections of someone as gentle and sweet as Brooke while alienating practically everyone else on the island, Kaylee couldn't even begin to guess.

Of course Brooke was also two different people. James probably saw the real her, while she had to play the role of her cousin to others, being the person they expected her to be instead of the person she really was.

In that sense, the two were perfect for each other.

"He told me I didn't know what I was talking about," Rick said. "That I was just trying to stir up trouble because I couldn't stand to see him happy. 'I'll give you the watch,' he said. 'I should have done it a long time ago. But don't you ever say anything to anyone about what you just said to me.'"

Rick slightly smiled at Brooke. "I didn't think James was capable of loving anyone but himself. That is, until he met you. But in the moments before he died, the only thing he cared about was protecting you."

Brooke closed her eyes, and tears spilled silently down her cheeks.

Kaylee stepped closer to Rick and kept her voice low. "You were there when he died?"

"I've relived it a thousand times. He drank from that mug, set it on the rail, and took off the watch. He turned it over, I suppose to read the engraving. 'Dare and endure,' he said. 'Wise words.' Then he took another drink from the mug and started to convulse. The watch dropped over the side and . . ."

Rick ran his hand over his eyes as if to erase a horrible memory. "He was dead. I couldn't believe it. That quickly, he was dead. So I left. As quick as I could, I left. I know I shouldn't have, but I panicked."

"You could have come forward," Kaylee said, trying to keep the recriminations from her voice. "You *should* have come forward. It would have saved everyone a lot of trouble."

"I was attempting to blackmail the guy. I was there when he died. I wasn't going to jail for something I didn't do."

"But you didn't care if I did," Brooke said bitterly.

"Not if you're the one who did it."

"Why do you think it's me?"

"Who else could it have been?"

Kaylee put up both hands as if to separate their accusations from each other. "Rick, you put the photograph of Alicia and Brooke on my door, didn't you? So I'd figure out the truth that Brooke was really her cousin."

"Someone else needed to know," Rick said.

"Maybe someone else does know," Kaylee said.

"The honey, the tea—it was meant for me," Brooke said bitterly. "Not James."

Rick gazed at the top of Brooke's bent head as he seemed to process then accept what she had said. "Then your life still may be in danger."

"That's what I'm afraid of," Kaylee said.

"Do you have any suspects?" Rick asked.

Kaylee shook her head. "I thought the initials on the watch were the key. Tyler Stevens said it wasn't his. Then Tim Slade was murdered before I could talk to him. Now I find out it's your watch, but all you were trying to do was get it back."

Kaylee ran her fingers through her hair in frustration. Now that they knew who the watch belonged to, it was no longer a key piece of evidence. The photographs weren't important either now that Kaylee knew who they belonged to and why Rick had them.

That left the oleander plant and the note Brooke had received asking her to go to the beekeeper's house. Someone had wanted her there so she would be accused of killing Tim Slade. It felt like the investigation was back to square one.

It all had to do with the honeyed tea.

Brooke's favorite drink, but not Beth's, not even when Beth took over Brooke's identity.

But had the murderer known that?

Kaylee didn't think so. But if Brooke—Beth—was the intended victim, as Kaylee had first thought, who wanted her dead?

And did they still want her dead?

18

A buzzer sounded and all three froze. Rick put his finger to his lips. "Stay quiet," he hissed. "I'm not going to jail because you're hiding out here."

Kaylee and Brooke nodded, and Rick disappeared into the front of his shop. Muted voices could be heard as he greeted someone, his voice cheerful and welcoming.

Brooke opened one of the albums and flipped through the pages without seeming to look at any of the photographs.

Kaylee decided she might as well do the same until Rick returned. "What will you do now?" she asked, keeping her voice low.

Brooke shrugged. "Until someone else is arrested, the sheriff will keep looking for me. I need to get off this island."

Kaylee thought of her boat, the *KayBea*, down at the marina. It had been Grandpa's boat, and he had named it for his "two favorite girls," Kaylee and Bea. After she moved here, Kaylee had taken the online classes offered by the United States Power Squadrons. Reese, a certified instructor, had given her the training she needed to get her license.

The fact remained that if she helped Brooke escape, she could go to jail. It didn't matter that Brooke was innocent.

Of course she could already be in trouble since Brooke had spent the night—two nights—at The Flower Patch. Would the sheriff believe she hadn't known Brooke was there?

Brooke must have seen the doubt and indecision flickering across Kaylee's face because she put her hand on Kaylee's arm and gave her a small smile. "I don't want you to get into trouble," she whispered. "Like I said before, just knowing you believe me means more than you can know."

"I'm not the only one," Kaylee said. "Kathy believes you. So does Jess."

Brooke's warm smile didn't dispel the sadness in her eyes. "You're right," she said. "I have more friends than I realized. But I can't have any of you getting into trouble because of me. I need to figure this out on my own."

"How are you going to do that?"

"I don't know yet. But I'll think of something." She turned back to the photo albums.

More than anything in the world, Kaylee wanted to help Brooke. Besides, if Brooke had been the intended victim all along, then she could still be in danger. Would the murderer be satisfied with having ruined Brooke's life?

Until the true killer was found, Brooke was a fugitive. Now she wasn't only hiding from her stalker ex, but from the law and potentially the person who had murdered her fiancé. Who could live like that?

Kaylee glanced at the photo album page that apparently had held the picture of the real Brooke and Alicia in front of their mural, given the empty space on the page. Additional photos of the mural, including close-ups of different sections, were also displayed on the opposite page and a few subsequent ones. While she tried to come up with the best way to help Brooke out of this mess, she studied the photos.

One enlarged photo showed the lighthouse that Brooke, the original Brooke, had painted. Kaylee ran her finger across the photograph, noting the attention to detail and color. No wonder the judge had been impressed. The next photograph showed the shoreline adorned with plants and shells. This must have been Alicia's work. Though it also showed promise, the style was different. Perhaps that was why the girls hadn't won—they had each followed their own instincts instead of committing to a cohesive look for the entire mural.

Kaylee looked at another photograph of the shore-themed imagery. Something about the design of the flowers seemed familiar.

Before she could come up with why, Rick returned.

"I put up the 'Closed' sign," he said. "We won't be interrupted again."

"I'm sorry you had to do that," Kaylee said. Now that she owned a small business, she was more sympathetic to the demands of being a sole proprietor. At least she had Mary Bishop to help her out. Rick apparently didn't have any employees.

He shrugged carelessly. "Folks around here know I only keep regular hours during the peak of tourist season. And sometimes not even then."

Kaylee wasn't sure whether that was another stab at her supposed outsider status, but she decided to let it go. If Rick wanted to think of her as an outsider, that was his problem, not hers.

"We should go," she said. "Then you wouldn't have to close."

"Go where?" Rick looked pointedly at Brooke. "You can't go home or to the Stratford estate."

"I know," Brooke said. "But it's best if neither of you know where I hide out next."

"I have a boat," Kaylee heard herself say.

"No." Brooke shook her head firmly. "I'm not involving you any more than I already have. Besides," she said, looking sheepish. "I hate to admit this, but I don't know how to drive a boat."

Rick groaned. "You're an island kid. How did that happen?"

"My grandmother didn't have a boat, and Bee and I never learned." Brooke's expression saddened. "James was going to teach me. But now . . ."

"I could take you off the island," Rick offered with only a slight note of reluctance in his tone.

"No," Brooke said firmly. "Whatever I do I have to do on my own."

"'Dare and endure.'" Rick spoke with more conviction. "I'm willing to take the risk."

"Why?" Brooke asked. "You and James were never friends. And he was wrong to keep your watch. I'm sorry he did."

"You're right about James and me. But your cousin was always nice to me. We talked about art every so often, and, well, I guess I had kind of a puppy-dog crush on her." He rubbed his neck. "I admit I was a little surprised when you seemed to give me the brush-off when you came back."

"I didn't mean to be unkind," Brooke said. "I was just afraid of slipping up. It's not easy pretending to be someone else."

"I suppose not," Rick said. "Anyway, you can stay here for a day or two as long as you don't go wandering outside." He glanced at Kaylee. "In the meantime, maybe we can figure something out."

"I suppose we could go over the evidence again," Kaylee said, though she wasn't sure herself how much good that would do. "There isn't much to go on, I'm afraid. Even less now that we know the photographs and the watch have nothing to do with the case."

"What do you have?" Rick asked.

Brooke quietly groaned. "I don't think I can do this again. I've been over everything and it doesn't do any good."

"Maybe you need fresh eyes." Rick grabbed a notepad and pen. "What evidence does the sheriff have?"

"Kaylee can tell you that," Brooke said. "Where's your ladies' room?"

Rick pointed the pen toward the door. "Down the hall, on the right."

"Thanks." Brooke grabbed her bag and left the room.

"Okay, Kaylee," Rick said. "Let's get started."

Before answering, Kaylee waited until she actually saw Brooke enter the restroom instead of making a break for it. She might have slipped away once before, but not this time.

"The dregs in James's travel mug contained pieces of an oleander plant," she said, glancing from Rick to the hallway and back again. "So did Brooke's honey jar, the one she carries with her. And then the sheriff found an oleander plant in Brooke's house."

Rick scribbled on the pad. "You're right. It's not much. What about the evidence in the Slade murder?"

"There's the note that lured Brooke out to his farm and the oleander plant found beneath his kitchen sink."

"Any ideas what it all means?"

"I think the murderer tried to frame Brooke, then killed Mr. Slade because he knew the honey jar didn't have oleander in it when he sold it."

"That doesn't seem like much of a reason."

"Mr. Slade would know who else had bought honey in one of those tiny jars." Kaylee's brow furrowed in thought. "It was also another way to frame Brooke. The evidence is circumstantial, and Tyler Stevens made it clear that Brooke wasn't going to be convicted of James's murder. But now she's suspected of killing two people."

Rick tapped his pen against the notepad. "Why leave the plants in both places?" he said almost to himself. "You found Brooke at that murder scene, right? So there was no need to put a plant there too."

"Maybe the murderer wanted it to look like Brooke and Mr. Slade worked together to poison James. Then Brooke killed Mr. Slade to tie up loose ends." Kaylee shook her head. "That sounds like something from a B movie. It's all so confusing."

"I agree." Rick looked at his list. "Is this everything? Sometimes the police hold back information to trap the killer."

"Everything I know." Kaylee glanced at Rick. It seemed strange that she and this moody artist had become allies in their united effort to prove Brooke's innocence.

"Sheriff Maddox tried to keep the oleander a secret," she said, "but it wasn't possible. Once the plant was discovered in Brooke's house, too many people knew about it. If he has anything else, I'd be surprised."

"What about witness testimonies? Did Brooke make a statement?"

"Probably more than one." Kaylee bit her lip in thought. "I talked to her about that morning. What she and James did before coming to the lighthouse. But it wasn't much help."

"I was at the diner when they came in," Rick said. "I'd taken the portrait out to the lighthouse earlier and was telling Alicia about it."

"Brooke didn't tell me that."

"No reason why she should. It seemed everyone in the diner was determined to kowtow to the great James Stratford. You'd have thought he was some kind of celebrity instead of the island's biggest jerk."

"Why was that?"

Rick rubbed his thumb across his fingertips. "Money. He has it. Or had it, I guess I should say. And other people wanted it. Didn't matter whether or not they liked him. They wanted to do business with him, wanted to be seen as his friend."

"But not you."

"Just seeing him wearing my watch . . ." Rick curled his lip in disgust. "I stuck around the diner as long as I could stomach it. I wondered for the umpteenth time whether he knew who he was really marrying." He hung his head.

Kaylee resisted the impulse to respond. Her instincts told her that he'd keep talking if she didn't break the silence.

After a couple of seconds, he raised his eyes to hers. "I didn't want to confront him there. Not in front of everybody. So I left the diner to come back here. The picture of Brooke and Beth was here on this table where I'd left it. The more I looked at it, the angrier I got. So I called James, and we agreed to meet at the lighthouse widow's walk."

"You haven't told Sheriff Maddox any of this?" Kaylee asked.

Rick shook his head. "I know I didn't kill James. There's nothing I can tell the sheriff that will help him find out who did."

"You were with James when he died," Kaylee said. "Sheriff Maddox needs to know that."

"Are you going to tell him?"

"Only if you don't."

"What is your deal, Kaylee? Not everything that happens in Turtle Cove is your business, you know."

"But this is." Kaylee's face was flushed. Her patience with Rick's inexplicable snobbery had about reached its end. "Because you fled the scene, I had to see it. And Bear," she stopped and caught her breath as an unexpected sob threatened to choke her. "Bear almost died too."

Rick immediately looked contrite. His eyes softened and his shoulders slumped. "I never wanted that to happen," he said. "You're right. I should have stayed." He sighed. "You just don't know what it was like. We were always rivals, James and me. All through school. You'd think those days wouldn't matter anymore, not now that we're adults. But we could never seem to get past them."

Kaylee glanced down the hallway to the restroom door. Quickly, before Brooke could return, Kaylee asked softly, "Are you in love with Brooke?"

"No." Rick said dismissively as his eyes darted to the same door.

"What about the Brooke you once knew? The real Brooke." Kaylee asked, keeping her voice soft.

Rick stared at her in silence. Then he shrugged. "We were friends," he finally said. "But that's all. I respected her and cared about her. But I wasn't in love with her. And I certainly didn't love Beth."

"Are they that different from one another?"

"They were practically inseparable. They were almost exactly the same age, and more like sisters than cousins. They were each other's best friend. But they had their differences. Brooke was gentler, kinder. Maybe because she was so often sick herself. She was probably the most compassionate person I ever knew."

"And Beth?"

Rick glanced at the door again. "She was the stronger of the two. Very protective of Brooke, in fact." He gave a short chuckle. "Seems strange that Brooke ended up being the one to take care of Beth. Protecting her with her name was the kind of selfless thing Brooke would do, though."

"Will you keep their secret?"

Rick stared at Kaylee. "For Brooke's sake, I will. Beth—our new Brooke—has nothing to fear from me."

"I'm sure she'll be glad to know that." Kaylee frowned as she looked toward the door again. "She sure has been gone awhile."

Kaylee and Rick glanced at each other, then both headed through the door. Rick led the way to the restroom and Kaylee knocked on the door.

"Brooke? Are you okay?"

Silence.

Kaylee tried the door but it was locked. She knocked again. "Brooke! Answer me."

Rick rushed to his office then returned with the key and handed it to Kaylee. "You better go in."

Kaylee unlocked the door, peered inside the bathroom, and pushed the door open for Rick to see.

The bathroom was empty.

The window was open.

Brooke was gone.

19

Kaylee followed Rick to the back door of his gallery, and they both looked up and down the alley. But Brooke had disappeared.

"Where do you think she went?" Rick asked.

"I have no idea," Kaylee said. "But she's resourceful. I suppose she'll hide someplace until she comes up with a plan."

"I would have helped her." Frustration edged Rick's voice. "She could have stayed at my place until we figured something out."

"Maybe that's where she went," Kaylee said hopefully. "Where's your place?"

Rick tilted his head toward the studio's second story. "Upstairs. It's convenient."

"Probably not there then. I think we should tell the sheriff. It's the right thing to do."

"You're not going to give up on that, are you?"

Kaylee shook her head. "He wants to find out the truth as much as we do. It's not like he only cares about closing the case."

"Are you sure?"

"Positive."

"I don't know," Rick said doubtfully. "Beth—Brooke—needs as much of a head start as we can give her. I think we should give her that. Unless you're afraid Sheriff Maddox will throw you in jail for not running straight to him."

"I hope he wouldn't do that."

"Guess it's time to see what you'll do for your friends, Kaylee, to see if you're truly one of us."

"Keeping information from Sheriff Maddox proves that?

We're not adolescents, Rick. And we're not talking about a juvenile prank."

"Compromise?"

"I'm listening."

Rick took a breath. "I tell the sheriff I was with James on the widow's walk, but we wait until tomorrow to tell him that Be—Brooke was here. Or that she spent the night at The Flower Patch."

Kaylee considered his offer. It could mean trouble for both of them, and she didn't like keeping anything from Sheriff Maddox. And yet, she didn't want Brooke to be picked up either. If only she could solve this case, then Brooke could come out of hiding.

"I could tell him myself. Without you."

"You could," Rick agreed. "Depends on who you're most loyal to, Sheriff Maddox or the new Brooke Edgars. You know it won't go well for her if you tell the sheriff now."

Kaylee sat on the back steps and crossed her arms over her knees. Rick was right, but she didn't like it. She wanted to earn Sheriff Maddox's respect just as she had the respect of the Seattle police department for her work with them as a forensic botanist, but she'd never been personally involved in the cases she'd worked there. She hadn't known the victims or the suspects.

Here in Turtle Cove, everything was different. Normally she'd be firmly on the side of law and order, but Brooke wasn't guilty of poisoning her fiancé or stabbing Tim Slade. Someone else had done that, and that person needed to be caught. Brooke shouldn't have to sit in a jail cell while the real murderer roamed Orcas Island.

"I have to find out who did this," Kaylee said. "And soon."

"Isn't there anyone you suspect?" Rick asked as he lowered himself beside her.

"No one." Kaylee stared, unseeing, at the backs of the houses across the alley. Then she focused on the visible side of a building a few lots down. She could barely make out the faint outlines of a painted scene.

"What happened to the murals?" she asked. "The ones painted that summer for the competition?"

Rick shrugged. "I think most of them were eventually painted over. They didn't hold up well to our harsh winter weather. Why?"

"I'd have liked to see the one painted by Brooke and Alicia."

"Again, why?"

"I don't know. Just curious, I guess."

"I probably have more photos in my archives. I could dig them out for you."

"I already saw them."

"The ones in the photo album? I think there are a few more in a file someplace."

"I'd like to see them," Kaylee said. "If you have the time to find them."

"I don't mind. That's what friends do for each other. Trade favors."

Kaylee didn't have to ask the favor he wanted from her. "I don't agree," she said. "Friends do what's right for each other."

"That's all I'm asking you to do for the new Brooke."

Trapped.

Though he probably hadn't done it on purpose, he'd set a snare for her and she'd walked right into it.

"Clever," she said.

"You'll give Brooke another day?"

"You'll talk to the sheriff?"

Rick pulled out his cell phone. "I'll call him right now. Do we have a deal?"

Kaylee took a deep breath, prayed she was doing the right thing, and nodded. "One more day."

Kaylee listened to Rick's side of the conversation with Aida as he made an appointment to meet with Sheriff Maddox later that day. After hanging up, he tapped the phone nervously against his knee.

"I'd ask you to go with me," he said. "You know, for moral support. But I don't think that's a good idea."

Kaylee shivered at the thought of Sheriff Maddox staring at her with his intense brown eyes. How could she avoid telling him about seeing Brooke if he was looking right at her? "I might let something slip."

"I know you don't think so," he said slowly, "but you're doing the right thing."

"If the sheriff arrests me, will you post my bail?" She was only half-joking.

He gave a harsh laugh. "No can do. I'll be in the cell right next to you."

They were both quiet. Kaylee broke the silence by saying, "You did the right thing, Rick."

"We'll see."

Kaylee brushed off the back of her pants as she stood. "I guess I should get back to The Flower Patch. With everything that's been going on, Mary has been working a lot of extra hours."

Rick climbed to his feet and thrust his phone into his pocket. "You won't tell her about Brooke, will you?"

"I won't tell anyone."

He nodded approval. "You're doing the right thing," he said, echoing her own words back to her. "It may not seem like it, but you are."

"Time will tell if you're right."

He suddenly grinned and extended his hand. "Dare and endure."

She hesitated only a second, then shook it. "Dare and endure."

After church the next day, Kaylee graciously refused an invitation to join Jessica and her family at the Pacific Street Diner, opting instead to spend the rest of the day going through her grandmother's photos.

She spent the afternoon and evening lost in history. The find of the day was a photo of a much younger Bea posing in front of The Flower Patch. On the back was a note in her grandmother's familiar script: *Grand opening of The Flower Patch, May 14, 1983. It's finally ready!*

Kaylee carefully set the photo aside, resolving to put it in the nicest frame she could find and display it in a prominent place in the shop. She would copy it of course, but the original should be in The Flower Patch.

The task was as distracting as she'd hoped, and her thoughts only rarely wandered into futile speculation about who the murderer was and where Brooke was hiding. At one point, she considered calling Rick to find out what had happened at his meeting with Sheriff Maddox, but she resisted the urge to dial his number. Sunday should be a day of rest, and they all needed a break from talk of murder.

Monday morning, she worked alone in The Flower Patch. Mary had put in more than her usual part-time hours the past couple of weeks and was taking a well-deserved break.

With Bear gnawing quietly on a chew toy in the doorway between the office and the showroom, Kaylee concentrated on catching up on her bookkeeping. All the order forms and invoices involved with the Stratford funeral needed to be entered into her accounting program. She idly wondered if it was wrong to hope that no customers came into the shop until she finished the task, since she was having enough trouble keeping her mind on the dollar amounts.

Her thoughts constantly turned to Brooke and Rick. She'd hoped to find Brooke in the kitchen when she came in this morning, just so she'd know where she was. But the place was empty. Kaylee had gone through the entire house just to be sure. But if Brooke had spent another night here, Kaylee could find no evidence she'd done so.

Where are you?

The question circled around and around, and she had to triple-check her numbers because she kept transposing them.

And then there was Rick. Maybe she should call him. Wouldn't he have called her if he had anything to tell her? Unless Sheriff Maddox had thrown him in jail.

But he couldn't have done that. Could he? Another question to disrupt her concentration.

A long hour passed as Kaylee continued to struggle with her bookkeeping, making almost no progress. She desperately needed a pick-me-up and perhaps a few minutes of conversation that had nothing to do with Brooke or Rick. Or flowers and math, for that matter.

"I'm going to pop over to Jess's for a few minutes," she said to Bear, "so you be a good boy while I'm gone."

Bear barked an affirmative reply before returning to his peanut butter toy.

Kaylee was almost to the front door when it opened and Rick walked in. Bear came running to greet the newcomer and was rewarded with a pat on the head and a scratch behind his ears.

"Rick, what are you doing here? How did it go yesterday?"

"Not that great," Rick said. "But at least I'm still a free man."

"Was the sheriff angry?"

"That's an understatement. Smoke billowed from his ears, flames blazed in his eyes. I haven't been told off like that in years."

"Did you find out anything new? Does he know Brooke is still on the island?"

Rick snorted. "Do you really think he'd tell me anything? I'm *persona non grata* as far as he's concerned. I imagine I'll be arrested if I so much as jaywalk across Main Street."

"I'm sorry."

"Don't be. His wife is a distant cousin, so he'll get over it." Rick gave a wry grin. "Someday."

Kaylee smiled, more because it was expected of her than because she felt any levity. *These days will pass. Someday they'll be nothing more than an unpleasant memory.* And hopefully, on that day, Rick and the sheriff would be reconciled, Brooke's stalker still wouldn't know where to find her, and the murderer would be in prison.

"I brought you a few photos of the mural I found." Rick handed her a file folder.

"You didn't have to do that," Kaylee protested.

"Tell you the truth, I didn't feel like doing much of anything after I got back from the sheriff's office. Browsing through a few archives sounded better than going for a run on the beach." He gave a wry smile. "Someone might see me and think I'm up to no good."

"You have no idea how often I wish I'd never gone up to the widow's walk that day."

"But you did. And now you can't stop asking questions, can you?"

Kaylee didn't know how to answer, if he even expected an answer, so she didn't respond. Instead she opened the file folder and gazed at the top photo, an 8 x 10 photograph of the mural painted by young Brooke and Alicia.

"They did a great job," she said. "Especially considering how young they were."

"They both had talent, but the competition was stiff."

"Who did win their age division?"

Rick blushed and dropped his gaze.

"You?"

"Yeah."

"Who was your partner?"

He gazed at her, his expression asking her to guess.

"Not James?"

"One of the rare incidents where we were a team instead of opponents."

"And you won?" Kaylee flipped through the photos. "Do you have a photo of your mural in here?"

"The last one. I thought you might want to see it."

Kaylee placed the last photo on top of the pile. The mural was breathtaking, a vista of boats on the sea and figures casting fishing lines from the wharves.

She took a closer look at one of the fishermen. "That's Grandpa."

Rick grinned, the first ear-to-ear grin Kaylee had ever seen on his face. "I thought you'd like that."

"This is wonderful." She looked at Rick with dismay. "Is it gone? I mean, did the store paint over it?"

"I'm afraid so. Like I said, the paint doesn't hold up to our island weather. It looked pretty awful after just a couple of years."

"I wish I could have seen it."

"You can keep that print if you'd like."

"You mean it?"

"Sure. I still have the negative."

"Thank you, Rick. This means so much to me."

"I hope it makes up for—well, I know I haven't exactly been on the welcoming committee since you got here."

"Why is that, by the way?" The question was out before she could stop it, and Kaylee winced.

But Rick answered honestly. "We get people who move here sometimes. They say they like the island lifestyle, the close-knit community. But then they want to change things to make it more like 'back home.' Folks from big cities are especially like that. So I wasn't too pleased when I heard that big-time university professor Kaylee Bleu had decided to buy up her grandmother's business and home. I've just been waiting for you to find fault with the way we do things around here. Start making your suggestions."

"I haven't done that. And I wouldn't. I used to visit my grandparents here when I was a child, and I love Turtle Cove just the way it is." She frowned. "Except for these murders."

"I misjudged you," Rick said. "For that, I apologize."

"Apology accepted."

Rick scooped up Bear who immediately licked his chin. "To show you I mean it, I'll do this little guy's portrait for free."

"I can't let you do that."

"I insist." He tickled Bear under the chin. "Who knows? It might start up a whole new enterprise. Pet portraits for the discriminating owner."

Rick's phone rang. He handed Bear to Kaylee, whose nose curled at the dachshund's peanut butter breath. She straightened his bow tie—a peppy combination of red, yellow, and green—while Rick answered his call.

His face paled as he listened to the voice on the other end. Kaylee stepped away to give him privacy, though her curiosity kept her from going too far. He was obviously distressed by something. He hung up and stared blankly around the shop, unseeing.

"Are you okay?" Kaylee asked. "Is it Brooke?"

"Her painting. I mean my painting of her," he stammered. He rubbed a hand over his face, as if trying to focus. "That was Aida Friedman."

"What happened?"

"Someone called the police. Said Brooke's portrait had been defaced at the lighthouse."

"Defaced? How?"

"I don't know." Rick looked around the shop as if unable to focus on anything. He finally looked at Kaylee. "Nick Durham is on his way to the keeper's cottage. He wants me to meet him there."

"I'll drive you."

"That's not necessary." He headed for the door but stumbled on his way.

"I think it is," Kaylee said. "I'll get my keys."

Within minutes, Kaylee had closed up The Flower Patch and strapped Bear into his seat, which she had moved to the backseat so Rick could sit up front. As soon as their seat belts were buckled, they were on their way to the lighthouse.

During the short drive, Rick stared out the passenger window in silence. Kaylee tried to imagine his thoughts, but she doubted she could understand how devastating this was for him. The portrait of Brooke had been a masterpiece, and the idea of someone defacing it was abominable. She tried to think of something to say, but any words of comfort she could come up with sounded too trite or insincere no matter how much she meant them.

Perhaps silence was best after all.

20

Kaylee had barely put the car in park before Rick flung open the car door and sprinted for the lighthouse. Kaylee unbuckled Bear and clutched him in her arms as she raced after Rick.

Deputy Nick Durham stood in the doorway and prevented Rick from entering. He raised his eyebrows as Kaylee drew near. "I didn't expect to see you here," he said.

"I was with Rick when he got Aida's call," Kaylee said. "How bad is it?"

"Let me in there." Rick's voice shook with anger. "I need to see it."

Nick held up his hands. "Just hold on a minute. Deputy Garcia is still taking a few photographs."

"Photographs?" Rick spouted.

"It may be a simple case of vandalism," Nick went on. "Probably a couple of kids who need a strong lesson in right and wrong. But the sheriff wants it treated like a crime scene in case it has anything to do with the murders we've had around here lately."

"How could it?" Rick practically spat the question.

"You'll see," Nick answered.

Kaylee held onto Bear while Rick paced in front of the lighthouse. Though it seemed like an eternity, only a few minutes passed before Deputy Garcia appeared beside Nick. They huddled together in a whispered conversation, then Nick gestured to the painter.

"You can go in now," he said.

Rick immediately followed Deputy Garcia into the lighthouse. Kaylee entered after them, though she wasn't sure the invitation included her. If the deputies didn't want her to see the painting, they'd have to say so. Nick looked like he was about to stop her, but then he must have changed his mind. Instead, he brought up the rear of the small group.

The portrait still stood on the easel where it had been since before the wedding date. One ugly word, painted in bright red with broad strokes, appeared across its width.

Murderer!

Kaylee gasped. "How awful!"

"Do you have any idea who did this?" Rick's voice, too steady and too in control, was more intimidating than his earlier outburst.

"Unfortunately, no," Deputy Garcia said, her tone brisk and professional. "I know this is difficult, Mr. Saunders. It could be directed at Brooke Edgars, an accusation against her. Or it might be someone who's upset with you. It could even be both. Do you have any enemies or know of anyone who has a grudge against you?"

"Not enough to do anything like this."

"Think about it," the deputy urged, handing him a card. "And if you come up with any names, please give us a call."

"Sure," Rick said dismissively. His entire attention seemed to be on the portrait. "I need to take this to my studio. Restore it before Brooke sees it."

Nick's expression brightened as his senses appeared to go on full alert. "You know where Brooke is?"

"I don't," Rick said coolly. "But she's gone through enough pain, don't you think? When she comes back to Turtle Cove, she doesn't need to see this."

"So you're saying she left Turtle Cove?"

"I would assume so. Otherwise wouldn't you have found her by now?" Rick raised an eyebrow insolently.

Nick worked his jaw, and Kaylee could imagine all the things he wanted to say. He was too much of a professional to respond to such a loaded question.

"We'll find her," he eventually said, his tone even and firm.

"I don't think she should see this either," Deputy Garcia piped up. "But I'm sorry, Mr. Saunders. We can't let you take it to your studio. The sheriff considers it evidence. I was hoping you could advise me on the best way to transport it to headquarters. We want to minimize any risk of damage. Well, more than has already been done."

Rick appeared to consider the request. "The packing crate is in the utility room. I left it there so it would be handy when it came time to take the portrait to the estate. I'll get it."

"I'll come with you," Deputy Garcia said.

After they left, Kaylee stepped closer to the painting and Nick joined her.

"I can't believe anyone would do this," she said. "It's horrible."

"No more so than poisoning James Stratford or stabbing Tim Slade."

Kaylee agreed with him, but all she could do was rest her chin on the top of Bear's head. His warmth within her arms gave her a comfort against the chill in the room.

"Can I ask you something, Kaylee?" Nick asked.

"Of course."

"Do you know where Brooke is?"

She didn't respond.

"Kaylee?"

This was her chance to confess, and she wouldn't be breaking her promise to Rick. It might not be quite twenty-four hours since they'd reached their compromise, but it was close enough. Even so, she couldn't summon the courage to tell Nick everything she knew.

"No," she said, consoling herself that she wasn't telling him a lie. "I don't."

"If you did, would you tell me?"

"I don't believe she killed James. Or Mr. Slade."

"That's not answering my question."

"She doesn't belong in jail."

"That's not up to you."

There was nothing else for her to say, so she said nothing. Nick sighed in frustration and Kaylee took a step closer to the portrait. Something about the exclamation point seemed odd. Except that the color was all wrong—a blood red instead of a vibrant purple—it resembled a stylized lavender blossom more than a punctuation mark. Though maybe that's what the vandal intended. The style tickled something in the back of her mind.

Beneath the lighting, the red paint glistened as if it was still damp.

"This couldn't have been done that long ago," she observed.

"You're right," Nick said. "Probably no more than an hour or so before we got the call."

"Who called?"

"It was anonymous. Maybe even disguised."

"That seems odd." Kaylee's mind whirled then quickly reached a conclusion—an almost too-obvious conclusion. "Perhaps it was the same person."

"The vandal and the informant?" Nick seemed to consider the possibility. "Why do you say that?"

"Anyone else would have given their name, probably even waited around for you to show up."

"Could be. Any ideas on who our vandal-slash-informant might be?"

"I wish," Kaylee said. "Because I think he's the killer too."

Kaylee offered to take Rick back to his studio, but he didn't want to be separated from his portrait before he absolutely had to be. He arranged to ride with Deputy Garcia to the sheriff's office, and she volunteered to bring him back to Turtle Cove.

Nick accompanied Kaylee to her car while Bear scampered among the plants leading from the lighthouse to the parking lot. It was hard to believe that less than two weeks ago the Petal Pushers had been busy getting the grounds spruced up for the wedding of the year. Instead, the lighthouse had gone from being a place of celebration to a crime scene.

A shiver raced up Kaylee's spine as a new thought occurred to her. What if Brooke's stalker was behind all the recent murder and mayhem? What if he'd figured out she wasn't actually dead and managed to track her to Turtle Cove? She wished she knew his name and his whereabouts. Maybe she could ask Kathy to get the information from Brooke.

But she didn't dare.

So far, Rick, Jessica, Kathy, and she were the only ones who knew Brooke's secret. Four people who had promised not to let her true identity become known. Not even Tyler Stevens had been told.

Brooke might think four people were four too many. If she managed to get off the island, would she ever return?

As Kaylee and Nick approached her car, she said, "Thanks again for driving me to the vet's office so quickly. I know it made a difference for Bear."

"You could make it up to me by having dinner with me," Nick said, a broad grin on his face. He scratched Bear's head. "I'm glad he's okay."

"Me too." Ignoring his flirtatious invitation, Kaylee opened the back door and strapped Bear into his harness.

"Well," she said, as she climbed in and started the ignition. "Let me know if I can do anything, I guess."

"Besides tell us where Brooke is? And is that a no on dinner?"

"I'll see you, Nick."

"I'll wait, Kaylee." He gave her his usual wink, then shut her door and waved as she pulled away. She glanced at him in the rearview mirror.

"What do you think, Bear?" she asked as she pulled onto the main road for Turtle Cove. "Should I have said yes to a date with Nick?"

Bear gave a sharp bark and Kaylee laughed.

"That's what I thought you'd say."

Kaylee found it difficult to settle down that evening. She brought her stacks of photos down from the attic and used her printer to scan the photographs for her nieces' albums. She'd give them the originals, but this way she'd have digital copies as a backup. When she had finished a shoebox of pictures, her shoulders ached from the repetitive motions.

A cup of tea before bed was just what she needed.

Kaylee set the kettle on the stove then walked outside with Bear. She never tired of the view of the back meadow, no matter the season, the time of day, or the weather. In quiet moments like this, she felt like the luckiest person in the world.

If everyone had a view like this, perhaps there'd be a lot less crime and hate and spite in the world. The sweet fragrance of the lavender, the fresh sea air, and the twinkling stars were a balm to her weary and troubled soul. Against this backdrop, she could pretend all was well in her world.

Once back inside, she fixed a cup of chamomile tea and noticed the folder she'd placed on the kitchen island when she arrived home. She sorted through the photos of the long-ago murals while sipping her tea.

She placed a photograph of the mural painted by Rick and James next to a photograph of the mural painted by Alicia and Brooke. The side-by-side comparison made it easy to see why the boys had won, and she doubted the judges had struggled to pick the winner.

The boys' mural had a vibrancy about it that was missing in the painting by the girls. Kaylee admitted to herself that she might be a little biased. Naturally, she'd prefer a mural that included a likeness of her grandfather and a few of his pals. But it was more than that. She truly felt like she could step into the painting and be part of the festive scene.

She shuffled through the rest of the photos, which depicted either entire murals or close-ups of specific sections.

The clock chimed eleven and she startled. It was later than she thought and she was exhausted after another harried day.

"Let's go to bed, Bear," she said as she stacked the photos and returned them to the folder. "Tomorrow is another day, even if I'm not Scarlett O'Hara."

Hopefully it would be a boring, uneventful one, with no more murdered bodies for her to find or fugitives to abet.

Kaylee slept fitfully. When the alarm blared, her brain was foggy and her body felt weary. Again, she'd dreamed of Brooke, stuck in a field of oleander and crying for help, but now Kaylee was the one sinking into a lake of honey. The dream left her feeling unsettled, as if she could put everything right again if she could only figure out how. The answer lay just beyond her consciousness, tantalizingly close yet out of reach.

She shooed Bear outside for his morning run while she showered and dressed. Not even the hot water washing over her or the habitual movements of her morning routine helped to alleviate the strange uneasiness she felt inside.

The Flower Patch only had a few orders to fill for the private memorial Tim Slade's sister had arranged. True to her word, Mary had insisted on purchasing one that she then designed. Brooke had also asked Kaylee to put something together from her. The other orders were from longtime residents, but it didn't seem like the reclusive beekeeper had many friends who mourned his passing.

While Kaylee waited for her coffee to brew, she listlessly flipped through Rick's folder of photos again. She turned over one, then another, and another.

She started to flip over another photo, but stopped and returned to the previous image.

This was the answer to the unsettled feeling that had haunted her dreams and her morning prep.

The stylized flowers in the mural scene, though unrefined, were reminiscent of the oleander included on the note that sent Brooke to the Slade farm and the lavender-inspired exclamation point on the defaced portrait.

Her body tensed and a knot formed in her stomach.

The same artist had painted them all.

21

Kaylee waited until she arrived at The Flower Patch to call Sheriff Maddox. She had needed the time it took to drive from the cottage to the Victorian mansion to think about a plan. With so little evidence to go on, it seemed the only hope of proving Brooke's innocence was to get the murderer to confess.

Kaylee thought she knew of a way to make that happen, but she also knew she'd have to convince Sheriff Maddox to allow her to get the confession before he made an official arrest. Without a confession, it was likely the murderer would never be brought to justice. In that scenario, suspicion would always surround Brooke, and the murders of James Stratford and Tim Slade would join the annals of unsolved crimes.

Sheriff Maddox didn't mind meeting with Kaylee in secret. He even seemed to enjoy her cloak-and-dagger machinations. Afraid the murderer would see them talking to one another, Kaylee came up with a plan for the sheriff to stop at Death by Chocolate for a morning cup of coffee. Then he snuck out the back door and met Kaylee at the back gate that separated the bakery from the flower shop.

Though slightly skeptical of her evidence, he compared the photos she had with the photos he'd brought with him of the note signed with the initials *T. S.* and of the defaced portrait.

"I see a resemblance," he said, reluctance tingeing his words. "But I'm not sure it's enough to charge someone with murder."

"That's why we need a confession."

"That could prove dangerous. I'm not in favor of risking a civilian's life when an interrogation could get the same result."

"But would it?" Kaylee asked. "Besides, I'm a forensic botanist, remember? A professional member of the law enforcement community."

"When it comes to identifying plants," Sheriff Maddox said. "Not for what amounts to undercover work."

"Just let me give it a try. You'll be close by, so nothing can go wrong."

His expression remained skeptical as he considered his options. Finally, his shoulders sagged as he visibly relented. "How exactly do you plan to get the confession, Ms. Bleu?"

They talked for a few more minutes as Kaylee laid out her plan and the sheriff made a few tweaks. After they settled on a time, he went back to the bakery while Kaylee returned to The Flower Patch.

Her step was lighter than it had been for several days, and her spirits were buoyed by what she was about to do.

Finally Brooke would be free to come out of hiding. And the real murderer would be arrested.

Kaylee arrived at the lighthouse keeper's cottage several minutes early. The wedding gifts were gone—packed and shipped, she supposed—and the long tables that held them had been put away. The spotlights above the repositioned easel were turned off so it stood in shadows, barely visible from the center of the room.

So much can be hidden in the shadows—literal or figurative. The thought sent a chill down Kaylee's spine.

James had been a ruthless businessman, but beneath his pride and arrogance was a heart capable of selfless love.

Brooke wasn't Brooke at all, but Beth, a young woman who had taken the identity of her beloved Bee after being terrorized by a relentless stalker.

It had turned out that even Tim Slade, the beekeeper, was more than a reclusive hermit. When his sister went through his desk as she prepared to take ownership of the land and honey business, she discovered he had sponsored several children at a Mexican orphanage.

Then there was the murderer—talented and ambitious, but still driven by childish jealousies.

Lost in her thoughts, Kaylee didn't hear the door open.

"Hi, Kaylee." The voice startled her. "What's so important that we had to meet out here?"

Kaylee gave a grim smile. "I know it's an inconvenience. But it seemed appropriate."

"Why's that?"

"Because I know what you did."

The fake smile on Alicia's face froze in place, a vivid red line against bloodless white skin. She quickly replaced it with a patient, condescending smile. "What do you think you know, Kaylee?"

"You switched the honey jars at the diner." Kaylee forced confidence into her voice. Now that she was face to face with Alicia, she was more nervous than she cared to admit. Though she didn't need to be afraid. Both Sheriff Maddox and Deputy Durham were hiding in the next room, listening intently to every word.

"In all the confusion, with everyone wanting to congratulate Brooke and James, it was easy, wasn't it? All you had to do was switch the jars when no one was looking and wait for Brooke to add the honey to her tea. Your mistake was thinking she would drink it. It must have been a blow to your plan when James died instead."

A flurry of emotions flitted across Alicia's face, enough for Kaylee to know she had said exactly the right words. Any doubt Kaylee might still have had of Alicia's guilt disappeared.

"That's quite a story."

"Not a story," Kaylee said firmly. "Just the facts."

"Facts require proof. And I'm sure you don't have any."

"But I do." Kaylee didn't say anything else, though it was hard not to. She knew that the best way to get Alicia talking was to say as little as possible. As much as the murderous wedding planner liked to hear her own voice, Kaylee was certain she'd fill any silence.

Alicia eyed her, malevolence blazing in her eyes, but Kaylee stayed composed—at least on the outside. Inside, she felt like her body had turned to mush and was pooling in her shoes. But her technique worked.

"Impossible," Alicia snapped, her arms folded across her chest. Nervous tension filled the space between them. "You couldn't know anything."

"Why did you do it?" Kaylee held up the photo of Alicia and Brooke as young girls. "You were friends once."

"Where did you get that?" Alicia grabbed at the photo but Kaylee instinctively pulled it away and stepped back.

"I saw close-up photos of the mural you painted," Kaylee said. "You had a distinctive style for drawing flowers."

Kaylee moved to the nook where the easel stood. She carefully shifted it then turned on the spotlights. They shone on Brooke's defaced portrait, returned from the sheriff's evidence room, and Kaylee gestured toward the odd exclamation point.

"You still do," she said quietly.

Two red splotches appeared on Alicia's pale cheeks and fear appeared in her eyes. "Th-that's not proof," she stuttered. Her voice shook.

Kaylee shifted her gaze from Alicia to the photo. Two young talented girls with dreams for the future that lay before them, dreams that would turn to tragedy. "You were friends," she repeated sadly.

Alicia snorted and her malevolence returned. "The happiest day of my life was when Brooke Edgars moved away from Turtle Cove," she said, practically spitting her words. "She should have stayed away."

"This is her home."

"She waltzed back in as if she'd never been gone," Alicia continued, her tone bitter and harsh, as if Kaylee hadn't spoken. "Except she avoided me. Even pretended she didn't remember some of the things we'd done together."

"That's not a reason—"

"And the single guys around here?" Alicia's voice cracked and she swiped at the sudden tears dampening her cheeks. "You'd think Brooke was the only available woman on the island. It was bad enough when Tyler Stevens started following her around like a puppy dog. But Brooke couldn't be satisfied with him."

Alicia glared at the defaced art. "That portrait should have been of me. It would have been of me if only Brooke hadn't come back."

"You and James?" Kaylee asked incredulously.

"Why not?" Alicia demanded. "And then she had the nerve to hire me as her wedding planner, for a wedding that should have been mine. I did my best, I really did. But she wasn't wife material for James. She didn't have the taste, the sophistication to be a Stratford."

"So you tried to poison her."

"What else was I supposed to do?" Alicia screeched.

The sheriff and the deputy burst into the room. Rage distorted Alicia's features, then her expression melted into despair. "Why didn't she drink it, Kaylee? Everyone knows Brooke loved her honeyed tea."

Alicia alternated between convulsive sobbing and a hysterical confession. As Kaylee had suspected, Alicia had placed the jar of poisoned honey in Brooke's bag when they were both at the diner the day before the wedding. She'd been horrified when James died instead and, in her panic, took frantic measures to put the blame on Brooke.

But when the oleander plant found in Brooke's garage wasn't enough for an arrest, Alicia grasped desperately at another straw. She decided to kill Tim Slade and frame Brooke by making sure she was there while his body was still warm. "She could leave her fingerprints and DNA all over him, you see," she said to Sheriff Maddox.

"What about the portrait?" the sheriff asked.

"You let Brooke get away." Alicia's eyes sparked with anger. "So I thought I'd make it obvious she was the only possible suspect. Besides," she continued, resuming her air of haughty sophistication, "does that portrait look like Brooke to you? I mean really. She's not at all that attractive. It's without a doubt the worst work Rick has ever done."

Alicia smoothed her skirt and tugged at the hem of the matching jacket. "I did his reputation a favor, but do you think he'll be grateful? No. Men never are, no matter how much you try to make them happy. But I could have been a good wife for James. I could have been the perfect Stratford, if he'd only given me a chance."

Kaylee's head spun as she tried to keep up with Alicia's logic. Maybe there was no keeping up with it.

Finally, Alicia seemed to run out of words, and her shoulders slumped wearily. Sheriff Maddox approached her and said simply, "Alicia, it's over."

Kaylee stood beside Nick, arms folded tight against her body, as the sheriff handcuffed Alicia and read her rights.

"Guess we got our man, or woman," Nick said quietly. "Thanks to you."

"I'm relieved." *Especially for Brooke's sake.* "But I wish I had been wrong."

"I know it's hard." His eye regained its usual twinkle. "How about giving me a chance to cheer you up? Dinner tonight, anywhere you want to go."

She managed a small smile. "The only guy I want to spend the evening with has four legs and floppy ears."

Nick grabbed his chest in an exaggerated gesture. "You're choosing Bear over me? That really hurts, Kaylee."

This time her smile was genuine. "I might not have had the chance if it hadn't been for you speeding him to the vet."

"Just doing my deputy duty."

"And for that, I'll always be grateful."

A few days later, Kaylee arrived early at The Flower Patch. She puttered around the showroom, making unnecessary tweaks here and there, then headed to the kitchen area to fix a cup of coffee. She walked through the door and jumped back with a shriek.

Brooke perched on the counter cradling a mug between her two hands. "Morning," she said with an impish grin.

Kaylee took a deep breath to calm her startled heart. "You're back."

"I'm back."

"Are you staying in Turtle Cove?"

Brooke shifted her gaze to the kitchen window and seemed captivated by the beam of sunlight shining through the panes. "I'm not sure it's safe," she said finally.

"I think it's the safest place you could be," Kaylee said. "Despite everything that's happened, only a few people know who you really are. Sheriff Maddox doesn't even know."

"You won't tell him?"

"I won't tell anyone."

"If it hadn't been for you, staying on this island wouldn't even be an option."

"I'm just glad it's all over."

"Me too." Brooke slid from the counter and then placed a silver object in Kaylee's hand. "I think it's past time I returned this."

"Grandma's key." Kaylee traced the grooves with her finger. "Are you sure you won't need this again?"

"I surely hope not."

"Me too. But just in case" . . . Kaylee returned the key to Brooke . . . "keep it." Maybe Reese didn't have to change those locks after all.

"I'm glad you moved to Turtle Cove, Kaylee. You belong here."

"So do you."

"Maybe. I need to get away for a while, to think."

"Where are you going?"

"I'm not sure. But I'll stay in touch if you'd like."

"Of course I would."

Brooke took a last sip of her coffee then set down the mug. "Thanks again, Kaylee. For everything."

"Be safe."

Brooke retrieved her bag from the table, and gave Kaylee a smile that didn't quite reach her eyes. With a wave, she disappeared out the back door.

Kaylee scooped up the little dog who had been lounging beside her feet. "It's over, Bear," she murmured near his long, silky ear. "And you and I are never leaving Turtle Cove."

She wandered from The Flower Patch's kitchen through the showroom and out onto the wide veranda.

"We're home."